OTHER TEAM REAPER NOVELS

LETHAL TENDER

A TEAM REAPER THRILLER

BRIAN DRAKE

BRENT TOWNS

WOLFPACK PUBLISHING
— EST 2013 —

Lethal Tender
A Team Reaper novel

Lethal Tender is a work of fiction. Any references to historical events, real people or real places are used fictitiously. Other names, characters, places and events are products of the author's imagination, and any resemblance to actual events, places or persons, living or dead, is entirely coincidental.

Published in the United States by Wolfpack Publishing, Las Vegas.

Wolfpack Publishing
6032 Wheat Penny Avenue
Las Vegas, NV 89122

wolfpackpublishing.com

Paperback ISBN 978-1-64119-929-2
Ebook ISBN 978-1-64119-928-5

LETHAL TENDER

PROLOGUE

Milan, Italy
The Past

Ariana Elenetti slid behind the wheel of the sleek black Mercedes for what would be her last few minutes alive. The engine started at the push of the starter, and she steered out of the garage into the night.

The headlamps sliced through the night as she followed the neighborhood road to the motorway. She would be early for her dinner date with Ceasario, and he'd probably be late because of his "business meeting". She didn't like to think about his business but had to admit it provided a luxurious lifestyle, the big house, the fancy Mercedes, and whatever else she needed.

Ariana Elenetti had picked out a blue dress, black stilettos, and her favorite diamond necklace for tonight. Bright red lipstick, her black hair cascading down her back. She looked as glamorous as she lived, and a tired Ceasario would certainly perk up as soon as he saw her.

Traffic light. She stopped. Heavy traffic on the road perpendicular to her. She had to make a left-hand turn. The motorway lay ahead after that. She left the radio off. She liked to listen to the rumble of the AMG engine and the burble from the exhaust ports.

Cross traffic slowed to a stop. Her light changed to green. She stepped on the accelerator and started into the intersection, turning the wheel left, aiming for the right lane ahead, and then the car lurched forward with a horrendous crash.

Ariana screamed as the car reached the intended right lane, but kept going, bumping the curb. An open field lay on the other side of the curb, and the Mercedes flipped and landed hard, overturning several times, each landing jolting the car and thrashing Ariana's body against the seat restraint. Airbags exploded all around.

The Mercedes stopped upright, Ariana slumped in the seat, head hanging over her chest. Way too low over her chest, as if her neck had broken.

When emergency crews finally arrived, there wasn't anything they could do except pry her body out of the car.

Ceasario Crisfulli said, "I don't mind you making money on the side, Primo. Why would I mind?"

Primo Malone was a small man compared to the taller Crisfulli, and his hands were shaking. They sat across from each other in the back room of a bar, a private room, the privacy guaranteed by not only the owner, who was a compatriot of Crisfulli's, but by the guard Ceasario had placed at the door.

"Well, I wasn't sure, you know—"

Crisfulli waved a hand. "It's hard to make a living these

days, I understand. You have not been disloyal to me, and that is commendable. Too many others would have tried to undercut me somehow."

"No, never."

"Then why are you shaking?"

"Why are you talking to me like this?"

Crisfulli cracked a grin. "I remember when I was in your position. When the boss called, it was never good. Right?"

Primo nodded.

Crisfulli sat back in the chair. The drug business was tough. Not only did one face the danger of law enforcement, where a bribe here and there might keep the heat off if applied to the right spot, but there was also the danger of competitors. Of people in the ranks who wanted a shot at the boss's chair. Treachery was everywhere.

Luckily, Crisfulli had, in Primo Malone, a loyal earner. Crisfulli liked to reward loyalty.

Ceasario Crisfulli wore his usual white suit. He liked to project a sense of purity in his business dealings, and the white suit filled that role.

As he examined the thumbnail on his right hand, the drug boss said, "We do have a problem, Primo, and I need your help to solve the problem."

"What is that?"

"These people you're working with on the side. They *are* trying to undercut us."

"Ceasario, I swear—"

"Primo. Don't worry. I know you meant no ill will. You had no idea. We've been watching them. They tell you one thing, then go and tell their bosses another thing. They're using you, Primo. Using you to get to me."

Primo Malone stopped shaking. "They're using ... *me*?"

"It's not a good feeling, is it?"

"No."

"Uh-huh. When is your next meeting with them?"

"This Friday. Here. This room."

"I don't think you'll mind if I join the meeting?"

"Of course not. Anything to stop this."

"They're trying to move in on our territory. They'll kill us all."

"Not if we kill them first, Ceasario."

Crisfulli smiled. He laughed. Primo didn't laugh, but he wasn't scared any longer, either. "I hate to interrupt your side income, Primo, so I'll increase your cut one percent."

Primo blinked in surprise. "That's more than fair."

Crisfulli stood up and buttoned his suit coat. "Till Friday."

"Yes," Primo Malone said.

Crisfulli opened the door. His guard turned sharply but relaxed when he saw the boss.

"I'm going to be late for dinner if we don't hurry," Crisfulli said to the guard. They moved quickly down the hallway, into the main area of the bar, and out the front door. Crisfulli did not acknowledge the bartender, his contact there.

Out to the street, into the car, a quick merge with traffic.

Ceasario Crisfulli sat in the back seat as his guard drove, smiling, pleased with himself. He'd often thought, when in a good mood, that he was pretty happy for a fellow who was going to die someday — naturally or otherwise. But then he had Ariana to look forward to, and she'd make any man forget his ultimate fate.

His cell phone rang. He pulled the Samsung out of his inside pocket.

"Yes?"

"Ceasario."

"Yes, Carlos."

"Ariana—"

Blood drained from Crisfulli's face as his number two told him of the car accident.

When Carlos finished, Crisfulli hung up and told the driver to take him to the hospital where Ariana had been taken.

His hands were shaking just like Primo Malone's had earlier.

The accident was no accident at all. He knew that. Deep down. He also knew who was responsible. Before even laying eyes on the body, Ceasario Crisfulli swore a vendetta against the man who had dared to cross him and took Ariana away.

CHAPTER 1

Somewhere in Mexico
The Present

"It has to be under the floor."

Mitch Storey cast a wary eye at the shorter man next to him. Both he and Greg Macedo were out of breath from digging up the yard surrounding the small hut, which, even with the open windows, had very little air circulation which only seemed to magnify the heat already outside. One couldn't very well call such a small place a house, although it had been lived in as such by a man who had recently been running for his life.

Now they were going to dig up the inside of the hut. There was nowhere else to look, as Macedo had noted, though Storey made no comment. Digging under the hut meant getting rid of the floor. Luckily, the floor was made up of flat boards with narrow gaps in between.

Nothing that a little more sweat wouldn't take care of.

Macedo knelt down, aimed for one of the gaps, it didn't

matter which, it was all coming up anyway, and smashed the hook of his hammer against the wood. Once he created a suitable hold, he began prying up the board.

"Come on," he said.

A hesitant Storey joined in the effort, the wooden floor snapping and popping apart rather easily. The builders had not planned for longevity when they hammered the structure together in the literal middle of nowhere of Northern Mexico. This wasn't a domicile to sustain somebody long term; it was exactly what it looked like, a place to hide for a short time while arranging for better accommodations. The rolling hills of the desert, dotted with the usual brush and cacti, wasn't a comfortable place to spend any time, brief or otherwise. It was the kind of spot you used only in a life-or-death situation. If you were running from the warriors of the anti-drug squad known as Team Reaper, it was exactly what you needed, off the radar, off the grid, the absolute last option.

Each wooden board cracked as they separated the planks from the base, and they set the boards behind them, being careful to avoid the sharp nails because the last thing they needed out here was a puncture wound and a tetanus infection. Soon the two former CIA agents looking for a buried stash of cartel drug money were not only drenched in sweat, their shirts gone, but they had trouble finding places to put the floorboards. The growing stack against the far wall looked on the verge of toppling over, so they started another stack in front of the first.

Macedo and Storey stopped after a while, sitting on the last section of floorboard, panting, sweaty, and taking sips of bottled water.

"We're almost done," Macedo said. He finished his

water and picked up a shovel from a corner. "I'll dig in these sections, you start over there, and we'll meet in the middle."

Storey wasn't in any mood to start again. They'd been searching for the map to the drug money for six weeks. The search had involved investigating several other homes and safehouses, finally culminating in this little hut, the last place to look. If they found the map pointing to the location of six million U.S. dollars, the reward would be well worth the effort, but only Superman had the unending strength required to maintain a non-stop search and demolition project.

"Dude," Storey said. "I need some time."

"You need to drop twenty pounds," Macedo said. "Mitch, we don't *have* time," he added, probably too loudly, as he started digging. The base of the hut consisted of horizontal boards connecting the outer edges of the building, below which was dirt. The divided sections made a perfect search grid.

Macedo dug, setting the dirt behind him as he moved up the length of the section, urging Storey to get off his keister and grab a shovel.

With their backs and arms aching and more piles of dirt growing, the pair eventually stopped when Storey hit something that went *clang*.

"Oh, wow," Storey said. His tiredness forgotten, Storey knelt and began attacking the dirt with his hands, Macedo standing by, urging him to hurry.

When Storey pulled a metal box from the soft dirt, he quickly brushed off the excess. "I think we found it."

"Outside, fast," Macedo said, leaping over the boards to the front door.

Storey joined him a moment later, Macedo bent over

with his hands on his knees, taking deep breaths of the fresh air.

Storey put the box on the ground and banged against the lock with the hook of a hammer, eventually breaking off the metal plate and lifting the lid.

"Not a very good lockbox," Macedo said.

"This was supposed to be a temporary hideout, remember? He never expected to get dragged to the U.S. for trial."

A folded sheet of paper sat inside the box, the silver interior pristine and unaffected by the long dirt nap the rest of the box had endured.

Storey grabbed the sheet of paper and, after spreading it out, let out a whistle.

"It's a map, all right."

"Where's the money?"

"Nassau."

Macedo clapped his hands. "Say hello to the best pension ever!"

Two automatic weapons cocked behind them.

Macedo and Storey froze. They knew the sound all too well. Both had been longtime employees of the Central Intelligence Agency, and neither had spent much time behind a desk. They were veterans of the Special Activities Division, the section of the CIA concerned with covert operations, and Macedo and Storey had participated in their fair share of dangerous missions, dodged their share of bullets, and shed blood for the United States.

When the World Wide Drug Initiative, otherwise known as Team Reaper, captured Chologos Cartel leader Jorge Sanchez several months ago, and his daughter failed to break him out of custody, the Mexican drug community collapsed on itself trying to take what was left of Sanchez's legacy.

While a rash of murders engulfed Northern Mexico, the territory of the Sanchez operation, rumors circulated about a stash of cash left behind by Sanchez as a safety net for when he evaded Team Reaper's pursuit for good. He never thought he'd be captured, but Reaper never left a job unfinished. Nobody knew where Sanchez had hidden the cash, but he allegedly left behind a map to help find it. For himself, that is. The map was never meant for anybody other than him, but somebody knew about it, and that same somebody talked, and word spread. Macedo and Storey, on leave from the CIA, wanted to find that map and find the money it was connected to in order to live out their future retirement in greater comfort than a government pension might allow. Maybe even make that retirement ten years earlier than the Agency required.

It was easy to find the location of the hut by following the trail of bodies, and leaving behind a few of their own. Neither Macedo or Storey were afraid of honest shooting, but it had to be on the QT. They weren't supposed to be in Mexico, and there'd be more than hell to pay if they were picked up for murder south of the border.

Now that they had the box, they'd achieved victory. But the sound of cocking weapons meant they were no longer alone. And probably done for.

Storey turned first, Macedo following. Neither had a weapon. They hadn't expected to be at the hut long enough to need a weapon, and their effort to avoid being tailed, hammered into every raw CIA recruit during the first week of training, had told them their trail was clear.

They shouldn't have *needed* weapons.

That was probably a fatal mistake.

Three men stood a few feet away, one of them wearing a white suit and a smile, the others in dark clothes and cradling short-barreled 9mm Colt SMGs, ugly black weapons based on the AR platform that were designed for spraying as much 9mm lead into an enemy force as possible. The 30-round stick magazines protruding from the forward receiver told the CIA pair they had a lot of lead to spray.

The trio certainly didn't appear to have hunting deer in mind.

The man in white said, "Hot day?"

It was hot, the sun beating down hard on the "middle of nowhere" Macedo and Storey had been digging. Their glistening torsos testified to the temperature.

"Stand up."

There didn't seem to be any choice. Storey rose first, followed by Macedo. Storey examined the man's face. He was tanned, but not Mexican. His features seemed more Sicilian than Hispanic. Possibly Mediterranean. Perfect English. Storey's mental mug file failed to register the man's identity.

"Toss the box," the man in white said.

"Come and get it," Storey replied.

"No," said the man in white. He snapped the fingers of his left hand.

The gunman to his left fired a three-round burst from the Colt SMG. The salvo exploded into Storey's left leg, opening the upper thigh above the knee. Blood spattered onto Macedo, who turned away to avoid the barrage, letting out a yell of his own. He fell onto the ground, kicking up dust as he scooted away to avoid his friend's falling body.

Macedo cursed at the man in white.

"You shouldn't have assumed you were in the clear, my friend. All of your tradecraft is useless when somebody like me knows the territory better." The man in white snapped the fingers of his right hand. The gunman on that side fired his weapon, the sudden blast echoing across the landscape, and the slugs ripped open Macedo's right leg, pinning the man to the ground, the blood mixing with the dirt to form a reddish-brown puddle.

The echo quickly faded in the unmoving air.

"Get the box," the man in white ordered, to neither gunman in particular.

The shooter on his left ran forward, grabbing the paper map and the box, placing the paper back inside and the closed box in his boss's hand.

"You two are lucky," the man in the white suit said. "I am not a mindless murderer. But you could have left the lock intact," he added. He admired that they didn't scream or make a fuss. "Such destruction is uncalled for, even for a crude piece such as this." To his men, "Let's get out of here."

The gunmen said nothing as they followed after their boss, their boots crunching on the ground.

When they were gone, Storey and Macedo finally let out the screams they'd been holding inside.

Somewhere over the French Alps

The light over the fuselage doorway turned from red to green, and John Kane jumped out of a perfectly good airplane.

His insulated jumpsuit blocked the harsh nighttime cold, but the icy blast on his neck chilled him deep. Goggles over his eyes contained built-in night-vision capability, and the ground below took on a greenish hue. As Kane fell through space, he scanned for a dot somewhere in the forest. Kane pulled the ripcord; the parachute billowed out of his pack, blossomed into a full canopy, and jolted him violently. His descent slowed. He grabbed the risers over his shoulders and continued looking for the dot.

One of his Team Reaper partners, Cara Billings, was supposed to be down there with the landing beacon. They faced a tense situation in the Alps. If something had happened to her—

He found it.

The dot appeared off to the right, in a small clearing. Kane pulled on the opposite riser and drifted in that direction. He'd land perhaps twenty yards in front of the beacon, but that was fine. Cara had made the rendezvous. Plenty of other obstacles remained.

Jumping into the massive region of the French Alps wasn't his idea of a good time, but there was no other way, and the job was personal. One of Kane's other teammates, Axe Burton, had been captured by members of a French drug network Team Reaper were in the process of tearing down. Kane had flown in from Paris, where he'd been coordinating the operation with the help of French federal authorities. Now his team needed him in the field.

A gust of wind kicked Kane left. He corrected with a pull on the right riser, keeping the beacon in sight. Cara was taking a huge risk. If Kane could see it, so could anybody else.

The beacon cut off as Kane neared the ground, which rushed up at a frightening rate. He pulled on the risers to slow the descent in the last second and bent his knees on impact. The jolt of landing rattled his bones. He stayed on his feet, quickly detaching the rig.

Kane ran across the hard-packed ground to the Chevy Suburban twenty yards ahead. The motor turned over. He jumped into the passenger seat and yanked off the goggles. His eyes took a moment to adjust to the sudden low light in the big people mover. He grinned at the woman behind the wheel.

Cara Billings, dressed in black, didn't return the smile. "You're late."

Kane didn't miss a beat. "The in-flight movie ran long," he said.

She snapped on the headlamps. The terrain looked treacherous, but the Suburban was more than capable of off-roading. Shadows concealed both dips and bumps.

"What's happening?" Kane asked.

"We still don't know where Axe is being held," Cara said. "The ski village is crawling with Caron's people too."

"Since it's off-season, can we identify the bad guys better?"

"You wish. There are a ton of full-time residents around here, plus tourists who prefer green grass to white snow."

Kane shrugged. "We've faced worse."

"But I don't think any adversary we've faced is as desperate as Caron."

"You might have a point there."

Aymard Caron was but a cog in the machine of the drug smuggling corridor between France and Italy, but he was a big cog. The corridor served not only the two originating nations, but Spain, Portugal, and parts of Eastern Europe, where they faced fierce competition from drug producers in the Balkans, who weren't afraid at all to step into French territory and do a little shooting.

The French-Italian Corridor grew out of the rubble of the French Connection of the '60s and '70s, where European organized crime sent heroin into the United States via several routes. Once U.S. authorities smashed the operations, it forced the Europeans to regroup. They tried to re-establish their market share in the U.S., but competition from Mexico and Colombia made the arena too crowded, so they focused on home territory.

Various factions battled for supremacy for several years, until they were united by what informants referred to as a "living legend" in the drug business. The White Wolf so named because of the huge amount of cocaine he'd moved not only across the ocean but throughout the European continent. It was the Wolf who established the French-Italian Corridor, a united drug cartel that fed the need for illicit narcotics across Europe. Europeans were no different than Americans; they craved the stuff, as much as they could get, and they didn't care who they had to step on to get a fix.

But nobody knew the identity of the White Wolf. Some doubted he truly existed. The "legend" had somehow learned to make himself invisible, working only through representatives and cut-outs.

But now, he was on Team Reaper's target list. A big red circle over a blank face. They'd put a picture over that face very soon.

To reach the White Wolf, as was the goal, Team Reaper had to shoot their way through his cronies. Aymard Caron was the first step on a bloody brick road that ended with the puppet master.

Kane asked, "Has the woman Axe was with been found?"

Cara remained focused on the terrain as she drove. "She's a ghost. Total ghost."

"Did you at least get a look at her?"

"Only a flash of blonde hair from across the other side

of the room. Before I knew it, Axe was arm-in-arm with her and leaving the restaurant."

Axe Burton loved the ladies. Probably a little too much, Kane always told him. He was one fellow that could never settle for one woman, despite his on-again-off-again-currently-off relationship with Brooke Reynolds, back at headquarters in El Paso, Texas, that many considered his attempt to end his skirt-chasing ways. The story Kane had heard prior to leaving Paris was that Axe met a lady in one of the village restaurants, and said lady lured him into a trap as soon as they left. Caron's troops grabbed him in an attempt to make Reaper back off. Caron thugs had delivered the ultimatum via courier in Paris: end the pursuit of Mr. Caron, or get Axe Burton back in little pieces.

Nobody threatened Kane's people.

Nobody.

First objective: rescue Axe. Second objective: take down Aymard Caron. Anything less than accomplishing both goals was unacceptable. The European syndicates needed to learn the hard way that playing games with Team Reaper didn't grant a reprieve; it meant they only died faster.

Finally, Cara left the bumpy off-road for a paved road, the Suburban jostling over the shoulder until the tires screeched upon meeting pavement. Kane finally relaxed. They'd reach the safehouse in about twenty minutes.

"How are you doing?" he asked Cara.

"Fine."

"How's Jimmy?"

"How's Mel?"

Kane sighed. There was only one answer to both questions: *the same.* Kane's sister Mel remained in a coma, hidden away for her own safety; ditto Cara's son Jimmy, minus the coma. It wasn't even worth pursuing the topic further, and Kane had to admit he was only filling the silence between them anyway.

The SUV's headlamps barely pierced the darkness ahead, and Kane felt like he was traveling through an abyss. He was glad it was the off-season. Dealing with snowy conditions while fighting for your life wasn't an extra complication the team needed.

But there was truly only one thing on his mind.

Axe.

He hadn't been forced to bury a teammate in a long time; he wasn't going to break the streak now.

"It's about time you got back," said Richard "Brick" Peters as Kane and Cara entered the safehouse, a narrow two-story cottage, full of hot air, and not simply because Brick was talking. The place was comfortably furnished, if bare as far as decorations, but equipped with heat and a large kitchen. It wasn't a place meant to stay inside all day. Renters usually spent most of the day on the slopes during ski season.

"Tell me you have something," Kane said.

Brick gestured for Kane and Cara to join Carlos Arenas at the kitchen table, where Arenas sat in front of a laptop with a color map picture displayed.

They were a motley pair. Peters, an ex-Navy SEAL, stood 6'3" with a shaved head and tattoos on his forearms and was big all over.

Carlos Arenas was wiry in comparison, with a square jaw and short-cropped hair. They were both dedicated fighters, and Kane couldn't imagine them not being part of the Team Reaper effort.

Arenas said, "We got a tip. An anonymous tip, but the

email said Axe is being held further up in the mountains, at this place here."

Arenas pointed to a mountain chalet, a large, one-story home with a lot of glass built on a flat section of a rocky hill, more granite massiveness behind it, with a sheer drop in front.

"Who sent the email?" Cara said.

"No idea," Brick said. "It's totally a trap, though. Which means Caron is getting anxious because we aren't turning tail."

"The question is," Kane asked, "do we fall into the trap, or not?"

"I don't see how we can refuse," Arenas said. "If that's really where Axe is being held, we have to try."

"And if it's not, we'll end up in a meat grinder," Cara said.

"We'll get that one way or another," Kane added. "They aren't going to leave a token force to guard Axe. They'll have the best-of-the-best standing by."

"This picture is all we have for now," said Brick. "Maybe a close-up recon is called for?"

"This is Caron's last stand," Kane said, his eyes still on the picture. He was aware of his teammates watching him, though. "I'll bet you money, marbles, or chalk that Axe truly *is* at this place, and Caron wants us all in one spot for a final showdown."

"I'm game," Cara said.

"But," Kane continued, "where in the house is Axe? If we strike without knowing that, we're kicking down every door and wasting a lot of time."

"We also may be too late," Brick said.

Nobody else spoke while exchanging uncomfortable glances.

"It's the elephant in the room, guys," Brick said. "If we're too slow, they can shoot Axe before we find him. If they haven't already."

"Axe is alive," Kane said. "Caron gets nothing out of this if Axe is dead. Plus, he'd have gloated over the body. No, Axe may be in bad shape, but he's still breathing."

"We're going in?" Cara asked.

"Don't worry, if they think it's only going to be the four of us, they have another thing coming."

"What are you thinking?"

"We have the entire anti-drug force of France on our side," Kane said.

"Are you sure they won't surrender when the shooting starts?" Arenas said.

Brick and Cara stifled a laugh. Kane shook his head at Arenas.

"I knew we wouldn't get through this meeting without *somebody* making that joke," said Kane.

The French anti-drug force known as OCRTIS — Office for the Repression of Illicit Drug Trafficking — had of late been under a cloud, with the arrest and conviction of their director for, unfortunately, conspiring with drug traffickers to flood France with cocaine and heroin. The chief had redirected anti-drug operations to benefit smugglers bringing contraband into the country, in exchange for money. Only money. And not money for his grandmother's hip operation, nothing so noble. The boss had only wanted money with which to line his pockets. The arrest was an embarrassment to French law enforcement, and the scandal and trial was kept as quiet as possible.

Kane had been working with the former chief's replacement, Luna Blaise, since the mission against the French-Italian Corridor began. He'd found her a capable boss, and one that knew the only way to restore OCRTIS to its former glory was to send her agents after the big fish, and not quit until those fish were hooked, gutted, and grilled.

She also had big brown eyes and a bright smile; Kane had to admit he was a little smitten with the French anti-drug boss.

"What do you need, Kane?"

John Kane spoke with Luna Blaise on his cell phone, holding a steaming mug of hot tea on the back deck of the safehouse. The area really came alive in the morning sunlight. The green field ahead, and magnificent mountains with jagged peaks beyond were a sight to behold, and enough to make a man wonder who had designed such wonder. Kane could only imagine what the area looked like during the proper ski season when snow dominated. He might have to come back and find out first-hand to keep his expert skier status up to date.

"As many assault troops as you can spare," Kane told her, "and choppers. We're going to need a fast getaway from Caron's place."

"You'll have them," Luna Blaise said.

Kane ended the call and stepped back inside to update Cara, Brick, and Arenas, as the trio ate breakfast around the kitchen table.

Cara said, "I talked to Thurston, too. She'll send a drone over to get an infrared scan. Maybe we can locate Axe that way."

"As long as Caron doesn't have a dungeon under the house," Kane said, "that should work fine."

"When do we go?" Brick asked.

"Tonight."

Kane left the kitchen to inspect his equipment in one of the second-floor bedrooms.

He knelt before his pack and checked for the usual gear, spare ammunition, his communications unit. Pistol and carbine were accounted for. He disassembled both the SIG-Sauer M17 9mm auto and the Heckler & Koch 416 carbine to oil the action mechanisms. Then he loaded magazines for both and put the mags in his equipment vest pouches.

Once more into the breach. This time to rescue a friend, which motivated John Kane like nothing else. He wanted his team back together, intact, and ready to finish the job.

Kane didn't want to go in without an up-close look at the chalet if nothing else to note the terrain first hand, so after breakfast, he and Brick climbed into the SUV and headed for Caron's mountain domicile while Cara and Arenas waited at the house for the results of the drone flight.

They followed a paved road through the lush green for an hour, passing plenty of traffic, and especially vehicles parked on the side of the road as tourists took pictures of the landscape. Presently they turned off-road, aiming for a mountain range about 32 kilometers away. Kane drove half that distance before pulling off in a cluster of pine trees. He and Brick weren't heavily armed, wearing only their SIG M17s concealed beneath jackets. This was a soft probe, not a hard hit. Kane's other gear consisted of a pair of high-powered binoculars.

Neither man spoke as they hiked the incline, the effort easy with the shape they were in, the grass brushing quietly against their boots. The chalet became visible, nestled at the top of a granite cliff. Kane and Brick took cover in some brush and Kane took out the binoculars.

The Swarovski EL Range 10x42 looked large even in Kane's big hands, but they might have been the Hubble telescope for the view they provided.

"What do you see?" Brick asked.

"A huge property tax bill."

Brick didn't laugh. "Any guards?"

"None out in the open. Some vehicles. Very clean windows all around. I bet they have a problem with birds smacking the glass."

"How's the back side?"

"Looks like it's right up against the rock. It keeps us from getting in that way, but it also keeps Caron from getting *out* that way. Only exit looks like the front, where the driveway meets a twisty road."

A small engine rumbled in the distance.

"Reaper—"

"I'm really surprised—"

Brick jabbed Kane's side. "We got incoming."

Kane dropped the binoculars and looked where Brick pointed as the engine sound grew in volume. He swung the Swarovskis and focused on two riders on ATVs with stubby Beretta M12 submachine guns across their backs.

"Did we trip something or is this a roving patrol?" Kane asked.

"Who cares." Brick took out his SIG-Sauer and clicked off the safety.

Kane stowed the binoculars and took out his own pistol.

"Don't shoot unless they see us," he said.

"You telling me you ain't itchin' for a fight?"

"Of course I am, but I'm also picking the fight." He looked around. The brush in which they hid provided concealment but no cover; the trees behind provided excellent cover and concealment, but they'd have to run from their current spot to get behind the thick trunks. Such a move would expose them for sure.

A fight here might bring down the rest of the troops, too.

They had to be cautious. And *fast*, should shooting actually start.

The two men riding the ATVs were thin, dark-haired, with wiry arms holding onto the controls of their four-wheel vehicles, each one lifting out of his seat a little when the ATVs hit a series of bumps. They moved at a slow pace, obviously a perimeter patrol. Caron must have owned more land than what the chalet was built on, and, certainly, they were far enough away from the ski village where Caron's men could operate with impunity.

Kane's grip tightened on the M17. Nuts with waiting. This patrol meant that any innocent hikers who wound up this far from the road were in danger; the threat against those not involved in Caron's business, or in Kane's, had to come to an end.

They had a chance to send a message, and the two goons would be the couriers.

Though Kane admitted, he didn't know how they'd communicate from the great beyond.

"Let's take 'em," Kane said.

"Got the guy on the right."

"Got lefty."

Kane and Brick sighted through the brush as the troops closed the distance to their position. Brick fired first, followed by Kane. Brick scored. The right-side rider pitched forward over his handlebars, the ATV careening up a rise only to topple over into the pathway of his partner. The second rider had to brake before colliding, and Kane's shot missed, splitting the air in front of the second rider's head. The second patrolman hopped off his ATV, running for cover as he also unlimbered his Beretta M12 and sprayed covering fire.

The shots zipped over Kane and Brick, snapping into trunks of the pine trees behind them.

"You slip or something?" Brick asked.

Kane ignored the remark and swung the SIG up in both hands, his elbows locked in a classic isosceles stance, firing two shots this time as the gunner dropped and rolled into tall grass. The rustling green revealed his position, so Kane fired at the gunner twice more. Brick fired his own rapid salvo, and this time they both scored, the 9mm slugs ripping into flesh and the dirt, the gunman no longer moving after the echo of the last shot faded.

"Let's get back to the safehouse," Kane said.

"He said ironically," Brick added. "If they have any idea where we are, that place won't be safe for long."

"We need to hurry."

They started back for the Suburban at a fast run.

CHAPTER 2

As prison cells went, at least this one had wall-to-wall carpeting.

But it was bereft of furniture, a bare room with white walls and off-white fluffy carpeting.

And Axe Burton was chained to the wall under a window, in a sitting position, with his arms outstretched, and raised slightly above his shoulders. His legs were free, and shifting his legs allowed some comfort, but his upper body was numb from being in its position for so long. He no longer felt his arms; he let them hang.

The window over his head wasn't barred. The window didn't need bars because the cuffs in which Axe's wrists resided were firmly bolted into the wall, four bolts total. Only the Incredible Hulk could rip those bolts out of the sheetrock.

The window at least gave him some light and let him keep somewhat track of the day. He'd been locked up for two days now, and so far, hadn't been abused. It seemed that Aymard Caron wanted him only for bait, not information.

His attention perked when he heard what sounded like

gunshots. Single shots, a full auto burst or two, more single shots. Then nothing. Was the cavalry on the way?

But a few more hours ticked by, and Axe heard no assault. No alarms. No troopers screaming as they ran to defend the chalet.

He had counted at least twenty men when the woman had brought him to the house, in a state in which she'd assumed him too groggy to determine the details of his environment.

As soon as they'd climbed into her car, the latest Lamborghini, she jabbed a needle into his arm. Axe's vision faded fast after that.

The hardest part about being locked in the room was knowing how he'd gotten there. Perhaps he'd let his little head do the thinking one too many times. He'd hate to admit that to the rest of the team, though, assuming he ever escaped this mess.

When the door of the room swung open, Axe wondered if this was one of his twice-a-day bathroom breaks.

Nope.

A middle-aged Frenchman entered, wearing casual clothes. His hair was slicked back, and the sun streaming in the room reflected off the shellac.

"Your friends have been to visit."

"Did they bring beer?"

"No, guns. They killed two of my men."

"You better call replacements, it means my guys are heading this way, and they're not leaving without me."

"I'm well aware, Monsieur Burton. That's the plan."

"It's a lousy plan."

"We shall see."

"We've wiped out most of your guys, Caron. What did you do, hire a bunch of street artists? Maybe one of those mimes that are all over Paris like jackrabbits in Texas?"

Caron glared.

Axe said, "This is it for you, and you know it. You either walk away the winner, or the person coming up after you puts you in the ground." Axe paused, then: "If there's anything left to put."

"I wonder what will be left of *you* after tonight, Monsieur Burton." Caron reached behind his back and took out a 9mm Glock-19. "Shall we see what you're made of?"

"Do it. Killing me won't change what happens tonight. Or tomorrow. Whenever my guys get here."

Caron crossed the bare floor and put the Glock an inch from Axe's head.

The barrel of the Austrian polymer pistol so popular with cops and special operators was black down the center. There was no way to see if a round was chambered or not, but the trigger was set forward, ready to be pulled, and that only happened when the slide was yanked back to throw a round into the chamber...

Axe held his breath and started to sweat as Caron grinned and pulled the trigger.

Click.

The gun was cocked but the chamber empty.

Axe let out the breath he'd been holding, his eyes unblinking as he stared at Caron.

"Lost your bravado?" the Frenchman asked.

"You wait," Axe said. "I'm going to kill you myself."

Caron laughed and put the Glock behind his back once again. "But I'm the one with the gun, Monsieur Burton. Don't forget that."

Caron started for the door. He was about the shut it behind him when Axe called out, "Hey!"

Caron leaned back into the room.

"I could really use a bathroom break about now."

Caron cursed and pulled the door shut.

Axe Burton let out a laugh.

Reaper HQ
El Paso, Texas

Brooke Reynolds glanced sideways at her UAV partner Pete Teller and asked, "Target in sight?"

"Big fat target in sight."

The pair sat at a twin UAV control station, with two small monitors situated below a large screen on each side. The big screen showed a camera's eye view. The camera was attached to a General Atomics MQ-1 Predator. Brooke, the pilot, operated the aircraft while Teller handled camera operation and weapon systems. The drone soared over the vicinity of the Caron chalet over the French Alps. The MQ-1 was a sleek aircraft that looked like something a large-scale model builder might assemble and display at an arts and crafts show, but it would require a big space for such a display. The aircraft was six feet high, with a wingspan of 14.8 meters, and eight meters in length. The technological marvels were remote controlled by expert operators like Reynolds and Teller at Reaper headquarters along with similarly trained Air Force pilots around the world.

Missile pylons under each wing contained two AGM-114N Hellfire II missiles, an air-to-surface weapon with a high-explosive anti-tank warhead. When the Predator wasn't flying a combat mission, cameras mounted in the bulbous nose and under the fuselage provided excellent aerial shots. The belly camera was the better of the two, taking clear enough to spot a pimple on a prom queen's nose. The nose camera was best for monitoring ever-changing weather patterns in the flight area.

This time, the belly camera was set for infrared, and the mission was to scan a target, not fire missiles at it.

With her right hand, Brooke gently, but firmly, moved a joystick to remote-control the MQ-1 into a left turn. To her, the most difficult part of flying remote-controlled aircraft was the delay in the video feed. She could maneuver the drone with her joystick, and the aircraft would bank or climb or dive right away. Because of the video fed encryption, there was a delay of a few seconds before the change showed on her screen. Pilots learned to adapt to the challenge quickly enough, but there were moments, still, when it seemed they'd miss a target because of the delay. When Team Reaper was on the ground and needed air support, the delay was quite frustrating.

She watched the turn indicators on one of the smaller monitors in front of her, noting the position of the drone's nose, its descending altitude as it turned, and where it flew in relation to the horizon. She pressed the left rudder at her feet, helping the drone further turn, adjusting the trim with another control switch to keep the nose lined up with the horizon.

When she reached the heading she wanted, Brooke let go of the left rudder and turned the stick a hair to the right, so the drone flew level once again, directly in line with the chalet.

"Over target," she said.

"Copy, over target."

Teller activated the camera and started taking pictures.

They didn't want to keep the drone over the Alps for very long because of commercial air traffic nearby, so the first pass needed to be a home run.

Brooke kept a sharp eye on her instruments. Her mind was on the mission, but also thinking about Axe Burton.

Axe is in that house. Who knows what shape he's in?

Brooke Reynolds and Axe Burton had a relationship best described as on-again-off-again-mostly-off because Axe couldn't keep two things zipped: his mouth or his pants. Relationships were difficult enough; they were more so when somebody wouldn't stop talking and whipped out his dick at every opportunity like it was a new toy.

But still...

This mission was personal. She didn't hate the guy, and maybe getting shackled in a room because of a woman would force Axe to reconsider his ways.

She hoped so.

Brooke Reynolds wore her long dark hair tied back. She was tall, almost too tall for the UAV pilot chair at 6'2". Her towering height intimidated many a man, and somehow, she always wound up with bad boys like Axel Burton. Like it was a curse or something. It seemed like every eligible male in special ops had the same attitude as Axe, and it annoyed her to no end.

But they were good men despite the polish needed to make them right.

Teller angled the camera down as the drone flew over the target, Brooke slowing the engines, dropping flaps a few degrees, keeping the house centered in the camera frame as the remote aircraft passed over. Her indicators told her the camera was taking pictures in rapid succession, but nothing on the screen displayed the pictures. Only the chalet itself showed on the display, along with her heading, and other information needed to keep the drone in the air and on target. The infrared photographs, in their sharp digital format, were being fed to another server in the building, where the headquarters crew would sort out the best ones and send them on to Kane and the rest of the team. She wondered if she even wanted to see the shots. Because what if Axe wasn't there any longer? What if the only indication they found was that his body wasn't moving?

"Got 'em," Teller announced, keeping his voice steady, not betraying his thoughts. Brooke turned the engine to full power, raised the flaps, and climbed 4,572 meters to get out of commercial airspace.

French Alps
Team Reaper Safehouse

They were around the kitchen table again, Arenas sitting in front of the laptop, Kane standing behind him, and Cara and Brick sitting on either side.

Kane held his cell phone, with General Mary Thurston on the speakerphone.

"It's a one-story, as you well know," Thurston said, "and we have a main section, the big part on the east end, and then a narrow hallway leading to the west end. The house looks like a short thermometer if you look at it that way. It's at the west end, you'll see, where there is one infrared signature that appears stationary, but we can tell by the color code that this individual is still producing body heat."

"That has to be Axe," Kane said. "The bigger cluster on the west end is probably Caron and his gunners."

"Looks like eighteen of them, some outside, some inside," Thurston said.

"Used to be twenty," Cara quipped.

"We know Axe is alive," Thurston said, "so what are we waiting for?"

"These pictures," Kane said, glancing out the kitchen window at the fading sunlight. "Our friends from Paris should be at the staging area, and we'll make our move when the sun goes down."

"You need to stop talking to me," Thurston said, "and go get Axe."

"Yes, ma'am," Kane said. He ended the call and looked at his team, who turned eager eyes on him. "You heard the lady. Let's gear up."

Kane took the wheel of the Chevy Suburban while Cara rode shotgun and Brick and Arenas climbed into the back.

Their weapons and equipment sat in the back cargo area, under a tarp.

Kane steered the Suburban out of the driveway and onto the two-lane road, passing more cottages, most of which were empty. They were meeting Luna Blaise and her assault team outside the village, in an open field, where landing two military choppers wouldn't frighten the locals or the tourists.

Nobody spoke during the drive. They were dressed for battle, in full fatigues and combat webbing, but their weapons and communications gear rode in the back. Luckily the tinted windows would block their more than unusual attire from any innocent eyes.

Kane cleared the village area, heading for the countryside and then the first salvo of automatic weapons fire stitched across the hood of the Suburban.

The high-velocity bullets smacked solidly into the hood, ripping holes through the metal and continuing into the engine compartment. The interior lights blinked out, but the engine still ran — for a moment. The motor began to struggle as smoke drifted out of the bullet holes. A second burst impacted against the bulletproof windshield with a dull thud. Too bad the rest of the car wasn't as armored, Kane thought, as a third salvo aimed at the front tires shredded the rubber and sent the Suburban careening to the right. Kane fought the wheel, the back tires screeching as he fought to keep the vehicle on the pavement. "Hang on!" The SUV bumped onto the dirt shoulder, the front passenger wheel catching in a drainage ditch. The vehicle lurched, tumbling end-over-end into the green field off the roadside, each strike jolting Team Reaper in their seats. The seatbelts snapped taught to keep their bodies in the seats, while the heavy steel spaceframe crunched, bending under the pressure of each impact, glass splintering in a succession of rapid pops. Kane's vision spun as dizziness overtook him. One last tumble and the Chevy came to a rest on its wheels.

Kane groaned from the pressure of the seatbelt digging into his lap and chest. His vision still spun, and the left side of his head hurt as if it had been touched by the flame of a Bic lighter. The side airbags had deployed during the tumble, the inflated pillows accompanied by a slight smell of explosive charge. Kane felt around his body and didn't find any other injuries. Cara held a hand to the side of her and let out a short cry.

"How bad?" Kane asked.

"Banged it a little."

"We got incoming!" Arenas said from the back seat.

Kane looked. From the opposite side of the road, emerging from the brush, a group of at least six armed men, wearing ski masks, converged on the Suburban. They held SIG-Sauer SG 552 automatic rifles. And they obviously knew how to use them.

Kane, Cara, Brick, and Arenas struggled madly to get out of their seat restraints, the tight straps slowing their grabs for release buttons. Kane popped open his door, clawing for the M17 pistol on his right hip. He almost fell over, the dizziness not yet over. Bracing against the Suburban's driver's side doorframe, he started shooting, letting off two round bursts in the direction of the approaching enemy.

He'd loaded the SIG with a 20-round extension magazine full of Federal HST hollow-points, and the expanding hollow tip could turn flesh into hamburger without much effort as long as the bullets struck accurately.

Until his vision centered once again, he'd have to settle for straight-up covering fire.

"Get out, get out!" he shouted over the rapid blasts of the SIG-Sauer. The incoming shooters spread out, dropping and rolling into the tall grass, return fire peppering the SUV and zipping overhead. More gunfire on Kane's right, as Cara, braced alongside the front bumper, joined the fight.

"Brick and Carlos are getting the rifles!" she shouted.

"Cover me!"

Cara fired rapidly as Kane ran from the poor cover of the driver's door around the back of the Chevy, enemy fire licking at his heels. He turned sharply at the back bumper and almost tripped over Brick. The big man and Arenas had one of the gear bags open, HK rifles in their hands.

But there was a problem.

"We didn't load mags before we left," Brick said. "Rifles are useless. We're getting grenades."

"Hurry up!"

More enemy gunfire smacked into the Suburban, the vehicle rocking with each strike of 5.56mm fury. Cara ducked back as bits of glass and blown-off trim pieces pelted her. Kane dropped flat beside her, steadying his pistol in a cup-and-saucer hold, and fired twice at a Caron trooper jumping from concealment. The HST hollow-points smacked him in the chest, and he fell back.

Cara fired another three rounds, the hot spent casings striking Kane's left cheek. She shouted, "Reloading!" and scooted back. Kane moved forward to cover her while she slapped a fresh magazine into her pistol. Cara moved up again, Kane changing mags, closing the SIG's slide and lifting the gun to scan for more targets.

Two grenades sailed over the roof of the Suburban as the Caron troops rose for a charge, the explosive pineapples landing short of their position. That's all that was needed. The two grenades exploded, bright orange flashes of flame lighting up the field; deadly, razor-sharp shrapnel mercilessly ripped into the Caron fighters. Kane and Cara continued shooting as Brick and Arenas tossed two more bombs. Another pair of blasts. Kane and Cara ceased fire as the breeze cleared the smoke.

Cara started to rise. Kane pressed her down with his left hand while scanning the battlefield with the SIG in his right hand.

"Not yet."

But the threat level had dropped to zero. No enemy troops moved.

"Okay."

Kane removed his hand and Cara jumped up. Kane rose, dropping the half-empty mag in his pistol for his last spare, 21-rounds total.

Brick said, "Chopper!"

Kane pivoted in the direction Brick indicated but stopped short of bringing up the SIG once again.

"Ours," he said.

The French OCRTIS Leonardo AW109SP Grand New descended into the field, hovering a moment while three landing gears lowered, then settled on three wheels with a gentle bump. The rotor wash created a windstorm, but the engines began to wind down, the blades slowing to a stop. The side doors opened, and two people climbed out. They approached the shot-up Chevy and the Reaper team watching them.

Kane stepped forward with his right hand out.

"You know how to make an entrance," he said.

Luna Blaise wore a combat uniform that didn't hide her shapely figure, strands of dark hair escaping from under the helmet atop her head. Kane hoped he wasn't admiring her too obviously; when her eyes met his, he blinked and looked away.

"We heard the shooting. Looks like you didn't need any help."

"Almost," Kane said.

"Too bad," she said. "I was hoping for a little target practice before the main event."

Luna Blaise introduced the man beside her. "My second, Julian Berenger."

Kane had not met the man previously; they shook hands. He wore a combat uniform similar to his boss' but didn't look as good in fatigues as she did. They looked about the same age, though Berenger's face showed more lines than Luna's. He'd seen his share of action. Kane introduced the rest of his team.

Luna Blaise regarded the wrecked SUV with a raised eyebrow.

"Need a lift?"

"And some 9mm ammo," Kane said. "We about used up what's in our pistols."

"No problem. Get your gear and climb aboard."

Berenger helped carry the kit while Luna Blaise jumped back aboard the chopper to update the pilot and call a squad to take care of the bodies. The local constable would also require a friendly visit from the anti-drug agency over the incident in his territory. She told the Reaper crew not to worry; her people had a routine for this sort of thing.

The Leonardo's cabin provided enough room for Team Reaper's gear, and they settled into plush leather seats. The tan interior / black exterior of the chopper was a nice combination, and it was nice to travel in style. Each seat came with an attached headset so they could communicate. Kane's stomach lurched as the chopper rose sharply from the ground, the landing gear motors making a grinding noise as the wheels folded into the undercarriage, then the chopper climbed and tipped forward for the short flight to the next staging area.

If Aymard Caron thought a roadside ambush might bring an end to his problems with Kane and Company, he was wrong.

CHAPTER 3

They formed a simple plan.

Luna Blaise's Assault & Tactical Squad would begin the assault with a helicopter inserting on the chalet's driveway. Team Reaper would follow in a second chopper. They decided the best way to avoid being seen from a few miles out was to fly over the mountain behind the house, do a lazy circle while door gunners softened the target, and drop the ATS in the driveway first, followed by Team Reaper. The pilots said no problem. Kane thought the pilots were crazy. Conditions during the battle would dictate how and when Team Reaper had the chance to find Axe, but Kane made that his top priority and told Cara to stick with Luna's people during the assault.

The two choppers they used to depart the staging area was not the luxurious Leonardo helicopter they'd arrived with; instead, they lifted off in Airbus H175s, medium utility choppers complete with a door gunner on either side. The cabin seats had been cleared out to make room for troops, and Kane and his people, in the second chopper, sat in the open cabin, strapped to the forward and rear walls.

The choppers quickly reached cruising altitude and made their way to the Caron chalet. Kane and his crew were ready to fast-rope to the ground when the action started.

We're on the way, buddy, Kane thought, hoping Axe was holding up, as he looked out on the greenery below, the attentive door gunners sitting in front of their single-barrel machine guns. To Kane, the weapons looked like FN MAG 60-30 firing the 7.62x51mm NATO cartridge. Belt fed, with a red dot optic mounted on the receiver, all but the sighting system resembled a U.S. M-60 with which Kane and his crew were so familiar.

The pilots dipped low on the final stretch, flying map-of-the-earth over the terrain, angling upward with the final approach. Wind rushed into the cabin, chilling Kane even through his combat fatigues.

The first Airbus dropped over the edge of the mountain and swung wide with the chalet below, the left-side door gunner immediately opening fire at any target of opportunity. He sent heavy lead into a pair of cars in the driveway, flattening tires and turning the metal bodies into Swiss cheese. Then he strafed the main house, careful to avoid the section where they assumed Axe Burton was being held. The FN machine gun hammered over the whipping rotor blades, spitting flame and empty brass.

The first chopper hovered briefly over the driveway as the ATS team rappelled to the ground, head-to-toe in combat gear and Balaclava masks. Caron troops emerged from the house, and fired from ports in the windows, flame snapping from their weapons' muzzles. The door gunner returned fire, pouring lead into the chalet, breaking windows and knocking holes in walls. The ATS team fanned out, the muzzles of their bullpup FAMAS-G2 rifles spitting flame. The Airbus lifted away, making another circle to allow the second chopper to fill the space.

Kane shouted, "We're going in hot!" as their Airbus made its circle, door gunners firing on the enemy. The chopper hovered. Unlike the first, the second crew had to contend with an enemy force actively engaged in fighting back the invaders. Enemy fire smacked the chopper, whining off the open cabin door and passing dangerously close to Kane and his crew as they fast-roped to the ground, dropping like so many spiders, Black Widows looking for something to bite between their fangs.

The ATS team was moving into the main portion of the house, with Cara and Arenas following. Kane and Brick stayed together.

One item in their favor, Kane noticed as he ran for cover, enemy fire kicking up the ground around him, was that there was an entrance on the west end, with a small staircase leading to the door. The bad news was, two bad guys were coming out that door. One stayed atop the stairs and shouldered his weapon to fire, while the other hit the ground and ran for a cluster of trees. Kane fired at the running man, while Cara and Brick shot at targets firing from windows. The running trooper didn't fall; instead, he gained cover, and shot back, Kane rolling away. He stopped against a rock, which exploded as a shot from the Stair Gunner's AKM smacked into the surface. Kane yelped as bits of rock drilled into his left cheek and neck. He answered with a controlled burst from his Heckler & Koch 416 carbine, the 5.56mm tumblers quickly closing the distance between him and the Stair Gunner. His aim was a little off. The slugs splintered the wood of the staircase and the rail surrounding it, the gunner ducking back into the doorway. He fired again. The return blast cut the air over Kane's head.

"On your left!" Brick shouted as he dropped and rolled beside Kane.

"Take the guy on the stairs! I'm going for the trees."

"Copy."

Kane fired a covering burst, then rolled left and jumped to his feet as Brick's return fire kept the bad guys pinned.

John Kane kept low as he circled the outer area of the tree cluster, then started zigzagging through, discovering Caron's outdoor party area with tables and benches. *How lovely.* The gunner who had taken cover near the trees was directly across from Kane, perhaps five meters away. He saw Kane and let off a burst. Kane dived behind a set of chairs, wrought-iron jobs that weren't solid at all. *Lousy cover.* He answered with a blast from the HK 416, then rolled right, moving low through the trees once again. The shooter fired random bursts, having not seen Kane move. Kane closed the distance, finally stepping from cover about two meters away. The gunner turned to shoot, but Kane fired first. The salvo stitched through the gunner's chest and neck, sending him into an eternal dirt nap should anyone care to actually dig the punk a grave.

"Reaper One to Reaper Five. Brick, where you at?" Kane asked into his com unit.

"Your way into the house is clear, Reaper One."

"Heading that way, join me."

"Copy."

Kane ran, clearing the trees, heading for the side entrance with Brick Peters falling in alongside. Heavy fighting continued around the front of the house.

Cara on the radio: "Reaper Two to Reaper One."

"Go, Reaper Two."

"We're moving into the main house."

"Copy," Kane said. "We're going for Axe."

"Axe, copy."

Kane and Brick hopped up the stairs, stepping over the fallen gunner's body. They stopped on either side on the entrance. Kane looked, the muzzle of his rifle probing ahead.

"Clear."

He started forward, step by step, following along the left wall while Brick stayed right. There wasn't much distance between them. The hallway was a virtual bottleneck.

But the doorway to the room where the infrared photos indicated Caron had placed Axe was feet away. Kane moved quick.

"Slow down," Brick snapped.

Kane checked himself, stopped, took a breath. "Cover me while I check the door for explosives."

"Roger."

Brick advanced a few feet away from Kane, staying on the right wall. Kane knelt at the door, examining the knob close up. He let the HK fall on its sling while he removed the glove of his right hand and gently probed the gap between the door and the carpet.

"Axe?" he called out.

"Reaper?"

The voice was Axe and no mistake.

"Any bombs?"

"No, man, get in here."

Kane pulled on his glove again, took up the HK, and stepped back. "Coming in with Brick!" He sent an enraged kick into the door, splintering the frame where the deadbolt rested, the door swinging inward to slam against the opposite wall.

Kane entered with the HK at his shoulder, swung left, right. No threats.

"Did you bring a key?" Axe asked.

Kane regarded Axe a moment. He didn't look in bad shape, but he'd need a moment to get the circulation back in his arms before they exited.

Brick shouted, "They're coming down the hallway!" A full-auto burst from Brick's weapon followed.

They'd run out of time.

Aymard Caron had been pacing in his office space before the shooting started.

The large, circular portion of his chalet had been purposefully built to resemble the command center on his favorite science fiction television show because even drug dealers liked things other than selling drugs and cutting out the tongues of competitors. The room began in the center, where couches and large television were arranged, and moved upward on steps to other levels. Office, kitchen, library, assorted free space consisting mostly of windows that allowed the sun inside and also allowed one to gaze at the majesty that was the Alps.

He paced by his desk while the computer monitor situated there showed one of his compatriots in the syndicate. They were speaking over Skype.

When the first helicopter descended and started dropping troops, Caron turned off the computer and grabbed for a Brugger & Thomet MP9 machine pistol, the 9mm weapon charged with a 30-round magazine.

Through the windows looking out on the front of the chalet, he watched the black-clad commandos engage his forces, most of whom were still inside and firing out ports in the windows. Caron ran across the room to join his men there, flame blasting from the B&T. He watched one French trooper fall while another returned fire from cover, but by then Caron had hugged the floor. The rounds pierced the glass, creating neat holes in the thick pane that resisted shattering against small-arms ammunition impact, though the heavier caliber slugs from the choppers had taken out some of the panes already. Shards of glass twinkled on the carpet like diamonds.

The fighting continued, Caron moving from one window to the next, taking whatever potshot available to him. Emptying the MP9, he ran to a cabinet against a wall and swung the doors open, revealing more weapons set on a rack. From the selection, he snatched a CZ Scorpion EVO-3, a short-barreled 9mm weapon with a 7-inch barrel and 30-round magazine. Normally a semi-automatic and classified as a pistol, this EVO-3 was special, Caron having had the firing mechanism converted to full-auto. He grabbed two spare 30-round mags and stuffed them in his left pants pocket. The second chopper had delivered Team Reaper. He instinctively knew it was them. Who else? They were coming for their man Axe Burton. *Time to meet them halfway.*

Grabbing two of his men, he led them to the main hallway leading to other bedrooms. *There! At the end!* A Reaper trooper was going into Burton's room while another provided cover.

Caron opened fire with the EVO-3, the short barrel spitting a long flame. The Reaper trooper shouted something, stepping back as he fired, one of Caron's men taking the burst square in the chest. Caron felt blood spatter on his right arm. He fired again as the trooper ducked into the room where Axe Burton was shackled. The shots put craters in the wall.

Caron advanced, his other fighter beside him.

"We need something to put out those windows!"

Cara Billings stopped beside Luna Blaise as rounds cut the air overhead, snapping into trees, kicking up dirt around them. Luna agreed, and they provided covering fire while another OCRTIS agent worked his way forward and tossed a grenade. The explosive landed in front of the house, right below the main windows. The explosion shattered the panes into thick chunks that rained across the pavement, smoke pouring from the huge hole in the formerly pristine wall.

Cara radioed Kane with the update as the OCRTIS team rushed, firing as they ran, filling the hole and breaching the interior. Cara and Luna, along with Carlos Arenas, joined the fray. Cara shouted, "Reapers One and Five are down the hall with Reaper Four!"

The French unit and her own teammates responded in the affirmative.

Whoever built the circular section of the house, Cara thought, had a *Star Trek* fetish. The room resembled the bridge of the *Enterprise*. The remaining Caron troopers, overwhelmed by the rush of OCRTIS and Reaper, threw up their hands in surrender before they ended up bloodying the floor like some of their colleagues.

"Reaper One, Reaper Two," Cara said. No reply.

Gunfire erupted down the hallway.

"Reaper Three, on me!" Cara shouted. She and Arenas bolted across the room as Luna Blaise, and her people, secured the scene.

.   .   .

"Reaper One!"

Cara.

Kane said, "Go, Reaper Two."

"We're coming down the hall. Two bogeys heading your way."

"Keep 'em busy."

"Copy."

Brick stayed by the doorway as the shooting started again, the full-auto blasts deafening.

Kane went to Axe. "Close your eyes."

Axe shut them tight, and Kane reversed his HK 416 and used the stock to pound at the shackles bolted into the wall, once, twice.

"It's a plastic stock, Reaper!" Axe shouted. "You'll break the gun before anything else."

Kane stepped back. "Who's got the key?"

"The funny man down the hall I promised to kill."

"I'll see if we can help you keep that promise."

Brick shouted, "Look out!"

Kane hadn't noticed the gunfire in the hallway cease.

He turned sharply, bringing up his weapon, as Aymard Caron dived through the doorway and plowed his head into Brick's midsection. All that did was piss off the big man, who hit the carpet hard and let go of his HK long enough to smash his hands over both of Caron's ears.

Caron screamed, arching his back, which allowed Brick to throw the Frenchman off him. Caron rolled onto the floor, on his back.

Cara Billings appeared in the doorway. Two rounds spat from her HK 416. Caron's chest spurted red, and he lay still.

"Dammit, Cara!" Axe shouted.

Cara lowered her weapon with a frown.

Kane hurried to explain Axe's wish to shoot Caron himself as he patted the Frenchman's pockets for a key, found it, and released Axe from the shackles. Axe sat and flapped his arms to get the blood flowing again. "Crazy trigger-happy loon."

"Repeat that very slowly," Cara said, "and tell me what's wrong with that sentence. His eyes are open so he might still be breathing. Let him borrow your pistol, Kane."

"Cara," John Kane said.

"Seriously, if Axe is going to be a big baby about it after causing all this trouble, and after *we* risked *our* lives to rescue him, let him use your pistol as soon as his arms work again. Later on, we can patch the hole in his head where his brains are leaking out. What were you *thinking*, Axe?"

"Nothing appropriate for your virgin ears," Axe said, rising. His arms were working again despite the pins-and-needles. He took Kane's offered SIG-Sauer and held it over Caron's face.

The French drug runner's eyes were open, but if they comprehended Axe and the gun, there was no sign.

Axe lowered the pistol. "Hell with it." He handed the SIG back to Kane. "If he lives, let's see if he has any intel we can use."

"You giving orders now?" Kane put the gun away.

"Somebody's gotta do something productive around here," Axe said.

Cara said, "I haven't heard a *thank you* yet, Axe."

"That's what you get for taking away my kill, Cara."

To Kane, Cara asked, "Can I shoot him in the leg?"

"No."

"The foot?"

"Stop it, Cara."

"Big toe, *please*? What does he need both for?"

"I'm not telling you again, Cara."

"Left nut?"

"*Enough!* Let's get outside while Luna and her people get this mess sorted. It's still technically their operation."

Kane helped Axe out of the house and outside, the air singed with the scent of gunpowder and sudden death.

CHAPTER 4

Team Reaper HQ
El Paso, TX

Axe Burton sat in the doctor's office at Reaper HQ and decided that whoever invented the paper medical exam gown with the little tie things in back that were impossible to operate, so the gown remained open and exposed one's rear end for the world to see, deserved death more than Aymard Caron ever had.

No trial, no jury, only capture and immediate execution. Well, after two weeks of torture and blood transfusions to keep the dude alive.

"I'm fine," Axe said, as the team doctor poked and prodded him. The sound of his weight crinkling the white paper atop the exam table gave Axe flashbacks to his youth when such a noise signaled that an old bat of a nurse was coming in to give him shots. He'd hated needles ever since. He'd rather be up to his neck in cartel killers, out of ammo and relying on his fists, facing certain defeat, than have the tip of a needle anywhere near his skin.

The Reaper medical officer, Rosanna Morales, did not listen. Axe wondered if she ever listened to her patients, as the various protests of every member of Team Reaper and Bravo had gone unanswered with every check-up forced upon them by the brass, who seemed to have a "do as I say, not as I do" policy that kept them away from Morales and her paper exam gowns and her poking and prodding and probably her needles too.

Life wasn't fair.

"Tilt your head up," Dr. Morales said.

"I told you I'm fine."

"Tilt."

Axe let out a sigh and complied. *This is insane.*

Morales felt along his neck with gloved fingers, pressing here and there.

"Hurt?"

"No."

She moved down to his back and began pressing along his lower back, around the kidneys.

"Hurt?"

"No."

She punched him lightly. Axe groaned.

"Hurt?"

"What do you think? *No.*"

She said nothing as she moved around to the front again, but Axe detected a grunt. At least he'd gotten *some* reaction out of her.

Rosanna Morales was a recent addition to the World Wide Drug Initiative, otherwise known as Team Reaper. Early 30s, dark hair, big brown eyes. No family that Axe or anybody else knew of, and she'd made it clear from the beginning that she'd absolutely not step into the field. When asked why, she ignored the question.

She scoffed at the idea of ever touching a gun, but that made sense. She was a healer, not a destroyer. She didn't seem to mind helping the destroyers stay healthy, though. Axe wondered if there was some hypocrisy there but knew better than to ask. She didn't seem like the type to suffer fools, and even Axe knew a little of his personality went a long way with some people.

She wasn't hard to look at, though. Despite the stiff attitude she portrayed, she made sure her red lipstick matched her nail polish, that every strand of hair was in its proper place, and wore modest jewelry. If she played as hard as she worked, Axe figured she knew how to have a good time.

Problem was, he didn't think she'd ever have a good time with him.

So why bother trying?

She told him to lay flat, and he did so, while she felt around his stomach and sides.

"No pain?"

"Is the Pope Hindu?"

She frowned at him and finally stepped away, grabbing a clipboard from the nearby counter to make some notes. "You can sit up now."

Axe returned to a sitting position. The paper beneath him crinkled.

"Am I going to live?" he asked.

"Being a smartass isn't fatal," the doctor said, without looking up from the clipboard, "but it can be hazardous."

"What else?"

"You're fine." She looked at him. "Get some rest and take it easy a few days."

"I need to get back to the team, Doc. I can't sit still that long."

"Your choice. Nobody ever listens to their doctor, anyway."

"It's a thankless profession, isn't it? Good thing you make more money than the rest of us."

"You talk as if that makes a difference."

"Doesn't it?"

Morales let out another grunt and exited the exam room, leaving the door open.

Axe called after her, "Do I have to wear this thing all day?"

The doctor kept walking until Axe no longer saw her backside. He laughed and jumped off the table, grabbing his jeans from a corner chair. He tossed the paper gown on the floor, his bare feet cold on the tiled floor.

"You idiot."

He spun around. "Hey!"

Brooke Reynolds stood in the doorway with her arms folded.

"You ever knock? I'm not decent."

"Are you ever?"

"That's uncalled for."

"Calm down, I've seen your behind. And your tighty whities, which I've never understood."

"Because you don't think further than your nose." Axe put one leg through his jeans, then the other, quickly zipping. He maintained his grimace as he ran a belt through the loops of the jeans, then pulled on his shirt.

"Are we going to waste time arguing?"

"I didn't ask you to check on me, Brooke. Why are you here?"

"I wanted to see if you're okay."

"I'm okay."

"Are you sure?"

"Nothing that a dip in a hot tub won't fix. Want to join me? Swimsuits optional." He laughed. She didn't.

"If not you," Axe said, "maybe our very attractive and sociable doctor can find the time."

"You don't know when to quit, do you?"

Axe grabbed his jacket and held onto it in his right hand. "We can continue this discussion over a beer. Come on." He started forward, but she remained solidly in the doorway.

"I'm on duty."

"When has that ever stopped anybody?"

She glared at him and left the doorway with a curse.

Axe laughed and exited, going the opposite way. He wasn't going to chase after her if that's what she was thinking. Axe Burton didn't beg like a hungry dog looking for a treat. Typical Brooke Reynolds, though. Happier in front of her computer screens and control stick killing by remote control than anywhere else. No wonder they were mostly "off again".

A beer did sound good, though. And then a solid workout at the gym with the rest of the team, some target practice, and a massage later if the parlor down the street from HQ was still open. He might have a clean bill of health, but he felt kinks in his joints that needed to be rubbed out. He laughed at the phrasing. But there wouldn't be down-time for long. The fight against the French-Italian Corridor wasn't over by a long shot. When General Thurston sent them out on the next phase, he'd be ready.

He wanted to get back in the fight and fast.

. . .

"Caron will live," General Mary Thurston said.

"Nice shooting, Cara," Arenas snapped.

"And you were *where*, Carlos?" she asked.

"Settle down," ordered Thurston.

Arenas opened his mouth to reply anyway, but then caught Kane's look. Reaper One wasn't happy. When Daddy's not happy, nobody's happy. Arenas bit off his retort and only smiled instead.

They sat in the conference room at headquarters, including Axe Burton, who also, for once, kept his mouth shut.

"OCRTIS is cleaning up the loose ends," Thurston continued, "and it's pretty obvious what went wrong" — she glared at Axe — "but overall we can call the mission a success."

"Onto the next?" Kane asked.

"We're working on it," Thurston said. "Ferrero is on the phone now getting some things sorted, and he and I have to meet on our own to go over a few other matters. Why don't all of you take a day or two and relax, and we'll get on the next leg soon enough."

Brick was already out of his chair. "You don't have to tell me twice, ma'am."

All but Kane exited the room as if somebody had pulled the fire alarm.

Thurston remained standing at the head of the table, looking at Kane.

"Something on your mind?" she asked.

"Is Caron alive enough to talk?"

"Eventually."

"Did anybody ever find out where the anonymous tip that told us about the chalet came from?"

Thurston looked grim. "We don't know. That's what

Ferrero and I need to talk about. It might behoove us to find that source and learn why they decided to help."

"We thought, at first, the email about the chalet might be leading us into a trap," Kane said. "But we were wrong."

"What is your gut telling you now?"

"I have a feeling," Kane said, "somebody else in the syndicate has an agenda we're going to have to deal with. They needed Caron out of the way and used us to get the job done."

"I agree. We'll either trace the email or track down the sender the hard way."

Kane nodded and finally left his chair. "Good enough." He started for the exit.

"Get some rest, Reaper," Thurston said to his back.

"Maybe." Kane left the room.

Thurston studied the empty table. The room felt like a house with all the children gone, and she felt no shame in thinking of Team Reaper as her kids. She certainly cared for them as much but knew better than to let it show. In her early forties and single, despite her athletic build and long dark hair that captured more than its share of attention, she didn't have a family of her own to fuss over, so Team Reaper filled that role.

As the overall leader of Kane and the crew, the former US Ranger had seen her share of action, and she knew what the team went through in the field, probably more than they realized.

Axe hadn't said much during the meeting, not even a joke, and she appreciated that he might have realized the gravity of what he put the team through. His capture made a routine mission personal for them all, and when people like them became caught in an emotional experience that threatened their battlefield judgment, it exposed them to greater risk. They faced a bigger chance of failure, of getting killed, in that state. She'd have a private chat with Axe soon enough and explain to him the other side of the facts of life, that there was more to think about than himself. Right now, she was glad everybody was in one piece, Caron was in custody, and they could continue the mission.

They wouldn't always be so lucky, but Thurston put the thought away as she left the room to meet with Luis Ferrero.

The identity and agenda of the anonymous tipster wasn't the only thing on John Kane's mind.

The bartender placed a frosty mug full of beer in front of him, and Kane handed over a ten-dollar bill. He left the change on the bar. This wouldn't be his only beer for the day.

Prior to the meeting with General Thurston, Kane had sorted through the hourly intelligence reports that flooded Reaper headquarters, focusing on the last couple of days while they'd been overseas. One story from Mexico in particular, because Kane and his crew spent a lot of time working south of the border, jumped out at him.

And not in a good way.

The story involved the deaths of two American tourists in Matamoros, in the Mexican state of Tamaulipas, who were in the wrong place at the wrong time and killed in the crossfire of warring cartel soldiers.

The city had once been an easy-going tourist site not far from the Texas border, closer to Brownsville than El Paso, but close enough to travel to and from in a day.

But now the Zetas and split factions from the Gulf Cartel were fighting for supremacy. They didn't care who died. Kane knew of other Americans who had also been unlucky, some kidnapped and later murdered, others who vanished off the face of the earth, who probably saw something they shouldn't have and were liquidated.

All of it made Kane feel like he was wasting valuable time that he'd never get back.

He liked to think they were making the world safer by removing the cancer of the drug cartels, but the cancer kept growing, often faster than the scalpel needed to remove the malignant growth. Cases like the tourist deaths gave Kane reasons to think that they were not even making a dent in the issue, and it might be best to pack up, let the cancer grow, and try and find something else to do with his life that didn't require dodging bullets or watching good people die.

But how could he, knowing what he knew now, having seen the cancer up close, ever truly walk away?

But, also, how could he ever see any positive results from his efforts?

He finished the beer and ordered another, paying with his change. He was the only person in the bar at this early afternoon hour, so he only had his reflection in the bar mirror to contend with, and not the distraction of other patrons. He hoped somebody came in to use one of the three pool tables lined up behind him. Some billiards action sounded like the right prescription.

His cell phone rang. He answered without looking at the screen.

"Yeah?"

"Where you at?" Arenas asked.

"The bar down the street."

"We're going bowling, come along."

"Not in the mood right now, Carlos."

"You sure?"

"I'll catch up with you all later."

Kane ended the call before Arenas finished his farewell.

He spotted a discarded sports section a few stools down and grabbed the paper to take his mind off work, but it was always there in the back of his mind.

Kane left his beer on the counter and went to one of the pool tables. He racked the eight balls and started shooting for any pocket he could make. A nice distraction, and he felt his spirits rise as each shot scored right where he wanted.

A solution would find him.

As always.

In the meantime, he was a warrior. And warriors *fought*. Against the odds, if necessary, and sometimes, just sometimes, they even turned the odds around.

Luis Ferrero rocked back and forth in his office chair.

Thurston sat in front of his desk, her back straight, legs crossed. She thought for the umpteenth time that Ferrero needed to decorate his office and have some sort of a personal touch. The walls were bare; not even photos of siblings or parents adorned his desk, just the papers and accumulated clutter of all managers who rode a desk.

"How did the call go?" she said.

Ferrero had been on the phone with Luna Blaise of the French OCRTIS and therefore missed the after-action meeting.

"Caron is out of surgery and currently in intensive care. Blaise expects he'll be conscious in a few days, and then they can ask some questions."

Thurston nodded.

"What did the team have to say?" he said. Ferrero, codenamed Zero, was the operations leader of the World Wide Drug Initiative program. He had a solid build from time in the gym, because he'd once worked the field, too, and would not tolerate going to seed, no matter what his administrative position demanded. Average height, greying hair, single like Thurston. He'd served side-by-side with John Kane during a mission in Colombia once. He knew the war from the front lines, and that helped him do his job better than somebody who'd never fired a gun in anger.

"They're happy for a break, I think," Thurston said. "The thing with Burton really pushed them to the limit."

"We got lucky."

"I'll be having a private chat with him for sure."

Ferrero nodded. "Now," he said, "about this anonymous tip."

"Kane asked about that," Thurston said.

"Who's behind that email is something we need to learn."

"Right away, of course."

"Who might have wanted Caron taken out?"

"We'll have to go through the who's-who on the French-Italian syndicate. We won't lack for suspects."

"It makes me wonder."

"What?"

"If somebody is taking advantage of our operations and using us to do their dirty work. Billions of dollars are at stake, Mary."

"I'm well aware. Kane has the same idea."

"I told Luna Blaise we'd want to ask Caron those questions, and she'll let us know when he's ready to talk," Ferrero said. "In the meantime, let's get Slick on the job and see what he can dig up from cyberspace."

Thurston thought that was the perfect approach. Sam "Slick" Swift was part of Team Bravo, the headquarters crew that supported Reaper in the field. He was the man with the golden fingers, a thirty-something red-haired hacker and computer whiz. Nothing with a microchip was safe from his manipulation.

"I'll go see him," Thurston said.

"I want answers to these questions," Ferrero said, "before we continue operations against the syndicate. If we're being played, we need to stop that first."

Thurston agreed and left the office.

Ferrero continued rocking absently in his chair.

CHAPTER 5

Spirotiger Hospital
Chamonix, France

Adalene Severin hated hospitals.

She hated hospitals crawling with federal cops even more.

But the boss wanted information on where Aymard Caron was being treated, and reports on his condition, so it was Adalene's job, as the White Wolf's official representative, to get the information.

They knew one thing for sure. Somebody was trying to kill off the upper echelon of the French-Italian Corridor, presumably to take over. Adalene and her boss did not know that person's identity. Like the Wolf himself, their internal adversary was a mystery. The Wolf wanted to know, and so did Adalene, if only because discovering the adversary's identity would keep her out of the grave.

For a little while longer, anyway.

Because who was she kidding? The life expectancy of

upper-echelon syndicate operatives was never a long one — she might as well count her "golden years" on two fingers. She'd been lucky to reach her mid-30s as it was.

The people she killed to get to her position, as second to the White Wolf, hadn't been so lucky, or as fast with a pistol or other machinations of death. Adalene was an expert. She'd made her first kill at age 16. Nowadays, she barely touched a weapon herself. It was much easier directing others to do the killing, while she gave the orders.

For the hospital mission, she wore a white doctor's smock with appropriate identification as she roamed the hospital hallways. Nobody questioned her being there. Her shoes even squeaked on the highly-polished tiled floor in the hallways. *Clichés existed for a reason.*

Adalene received some curious looks, though, mostly from males who probably knew every female in the building and hadn't heard of any "new chicks" joining the staff. She smiled at the thought of remaining a mystery to them. They'd spend days after her departure trying to figure out who she was and when she'd be coming back. One or two looked a little too long. A quick evil eye from her set them back on their merry way, to whoever their next target might be, poor wretch.

The armed guards in front of Caron's hospital room had a checklist of "approved" doctors and nurses who were allowed to enter and check on the wounded man, and Adalene's name wasn't on the list, so getting close to Caron wasn't an option. Her crew could magically conjure up a smock and ID card, but they couldn't put her on that list. Such is life. One must make different arrangements in cases like that, and luckily, Adalene had a secret weapon.

Plain old office gossip. Employee chatter was better than electronic surveillance any day.

She sat in the break room with coffee and a physician's journal, reading absently about cancer research and advice about improving bedside manner when exhausted. The chair under her was a little wobbly, the table likewise, and she toyed with the idea of leveling out both with some sugar packets, but the gossip filling the room was second-to-none, so she ignored the wobbling.

Every time there was more than one other person in the room, they started talking, in hushed tones to start, then louder as the conversation became more animated, usually culminating in a joke punctuated by laughter meant to make it sound like they hadn't been gossiping at all. Adalene didn't miss a word. They didn't even notice she was there; at least, nothing about her presence kept them from jibber-jabbering.

Everybody on staff was talking about the "big drug dealer" in the secluded room, which normally had beds for two patients, but the extra bed had been moved out to make space for the federal officers and their gear. The men talked about how they didn't appreciate having to keep alive "somebody like him". The women talked about the good-looking cops in a hyper-sexualized fashion that all women denied ever speaking but did so when they thought nobody was listening.

The two guards outside changed every six hours. Doctors who made regular rounds into Caron's room, with their different attitudes than the male nurses and orderlies, said he was stable and improving, but they couldn't wait to get him out of the hospital and get rid of all the cops, too. The hard edges of their tones and harshness of their comments suggested to Adalene they didn't like cops or bad guys because of the trouble that came with both. She paid particular attention to when they thought Caron would be fit for travel. At least a week, and he'd still need attention, but the cops were talking about transporting him to Paris in two days' time.

Adalene Severin filed away the information. Caron could not, absolutely could *not*, remain in police custody. And it was a long drive to Paris, with plenty of spots along the way to intercept the police convoy. It was time to call in some specialists of her own to make sure he never reached Paris, but a syndicate safehouse instead. The White Wolf wasn't so much as worried about the Americans continuing their assault as he was the enemy within. They could not fight on two fronts. The internal enemy needed to be defeated before they'd have a chance against the group known as Team Reaper.

Adalene left her magazine and empty coffee cup on the table like any other hospital employee. One had to play the role to the hilt to convince the audience of being real.

El Paso, TX
Kane's Apartment

Shooting pool alone wasn't as fun as it should have been.

Kane eventually left the bar and returned home to his apartment, feeling beat. Locking the deadbolt, he hung his jacket on the coat rack near the door, which pitched a little under the weight of the jacket, since the four-legged stand only rested on the carpet. He promptly dropped onto the couch. He didn't bother looking in the refrigerator. There was nothing inside. He probably had ice in the freezer to chew on if he was desperate. The way he traveled, and often on short notice, he never attempted to keep anything that lasted more than a day or two, which meant only buying enough food to make meals for however long he was off-duty. During leave, he, of course, did a lot more shopping.

He'd simply been too worn out to make a stop on the way home. He decided if his stomach demanded something, he'd consult one of the two take-away menus near the phone, for the local Chinese place, or the local pizza place.

The couch was at least comfortable, a midsize affair with two fluffy cushions, though the two cushions seemed to sink in the center, creating what Kane called "the crack" where it was easy to sink so deep as to get stuck. He often needed to hook a foot under the coffee table for leverage when that happened.

The remote sat on the cushion beside him. He turned on the wall-mounted big screen.

And immediately wished he hadn't. Five hundred channels were great and all, except when *there was nothing to watch* on any of the channels, including sports. With a grunt, Kane turned off the television and enjoyed the relative silence for a moment. He heard muffled voices through the walls — his neighbors — but nothing loud enough to fully understand.

He thought about checking on Mel, his sister, but the hospital would have called if she had emerged from her coma. Thinking about her continued condition brought him down. Or maybe it was an after-effect of the beers. He wasn't *that* much of a lightweight, though. He had a lot on his mind, including his sister, and the load wasn't anything that might contribute to a cheerful mood.

His phone rang.

He reached for his shirt pocket, but the Samsung wasn't there. It was in his jacket. He hoped it wasn't HQ calling.

Rising, he retrieved his phone from the inside pocket of his jacket and frowned at the name on the screen.

"You're still alive?" he asked. A smile tugged at the corners of his mouth. Maybe this phone call would brighten the day.

"Dude!" the caller said. "What kind of question is that?"

Kane laughed. "A perfectly valid one, Don."

Don Mateo and John Kane went back all the way to the Marine Corps. They'd had neighboring cots in the barracks at Camp Pendleton during basic training and had forged a quick bond that neither time nor distance could break, and a relationship that cemented while dodging bullets in some of the world's hot spots with the Marine Force Recon.

Kane wandered back to the couch as he and Mateo caught up on each other's lives. Mateo was a "consultant" now, getting paid big bucks to tell companies how to improve their security and protect themselves from industrial espionage. He even engaged in some overseas "go-between" work when companies who operated overseas had to deal with pirates and terrorists holding employees for ransom. On that subject, he was pretty cagey, but Kane figured there was more than talking going on in those scenarios. Mateo would never ride a desk. He always had to be in the field where the action was.

His choice in a life partner mirrored his attitude. Kane had been best man when Don married a tall blonde named Katie, and her resume was almost as impressive as theirs with her stint in Air Force Intelligence which later led to contract CIA work and an up-close familiarity of the dirty side of espionage.

He surprised Kane midway through the conversation when he asked, "You still doing that anti-drug thing?"

"Yeah," Kane said. "With varying degrees of success, unfortunately."

"I hear ya. But, hey, I got something I need to talk to you about that's along those lines."

"Okay."

"Katie and me are in Nassau," Mateo said, "and there's something hot happening down here that you might want to take a look at."

"Like what?"

"Cartel dudes, dude. They're all over the place. I keep hearing the same rumors, too, that another cartel leader buried a bunch of money here before he was arrested. Did you have anything to do with the Jorge Sanchez case?"

"I'd rather not say."

"I thought you might, totally up your alley. Anyway, it's supposed to be his money. He stashed it while he was running from you guys, but you caught him before it ever came in handy."

"Very interesting. I hadn't heard anything about it previously."

"Well, I count five guys so far. One boss, and four big guys that are obviously gunners. They all trip the memory circuits in the mental mug file, you know?"

"Too well," Kane said.

Don Mateo had never worked for Team Reaper, but after Afghanistan, after the Marines, before becoming a consultant, he'd gone to work for a private military contractor who sent him and his team on an anti-drug operation in Colombia. Mateo knew the drill almost as well as Kane. If Don said there were cartel players in Nassau, it was information Kane accepted as fact.

"How long are you and Katie staying?"

"Another two weeks. Gotta love long vacations."

"All right. Let me do some research and talk to my boss, and I'll get back to you. Maybe I'll join you for a little sun and surf, and we can see what those goons are up to."

"Like the old days!"

"I'm too old for the old days," Kane said, but knew all he needed was a good night's sleep, and he'd be ready for more action after the sun came up. They said good-bye, and he ended the call.

Jorge Sanchez. Again. Would they ever be done with that case? Sanchez had been convicted after a three-month trial by a New York City jury and sentenced to life in prison. Kane had watched a closed-circuit television feed of the verdict, along with the rest of Team Reaper, who not only played a huge role in capturing Sanchez but also prevented his enraged daughter, Blanca, from breaking him out of custody by carrying out a series of terrorist attacks with the intent of making the president order her father's release. When the verdict was read in the court-room, Sanchez didn't blink or react in any tangible way. He'd been despondent since the death of his daughter, and Kane and Cara in particular, were surprised he hadn't found a way to end his own life, but Kane decided the man was too proud to exit that way. He'd spend whatever remained of that life behind bars, and accept his fate like a man.

Kane could almost respect a decision like that, even if he didn't approve of the man's existence. It was only under orders that Team Reaper didn't kill Sanchez when they'd had the opportunity.

Kane decided it was perfectly reasonable that Sanchez had stashed cash in Nassau, and, probably, elsewhere in the world, too. He'd been on the run for months, evading not only Reaper but US authorities in general, and would have had ample opportunity to secure cash at several hide sites, along with guns, and whatever else he might require.

Kane retrieved his laptop computer from the shelf under the coffee table, turning it on only to realize his battery was low. He found the cord on the floor under the couch and plugged the end of the cord into the computer.

He spent an hour researching what Don Mateo had told him, reading several articles about various rumors surrounding Jorge Sanchez and his hidden money. A variety of treasure hunters were on record as searching for the cash, not only in the Bahamas but elsewhere around the globe, but so far, nobody had discovered anything other than dead ends and frustration. Kane began to wonder if the story was simply a wild rumor, but if Mateo, who would know, had spotted cartel players in Nassau talking about the hidden money, perhaps somebody had finally discovered the location of Sanchez's loot. Which meant Nassau was about to become a powder keg. Which meant it might be the perfect spot for Team Reaper to investigate.

And a great way to get him to quit being a sourpuss.

At least until HQ continued with the remainder of the European mission.

The thought made Kane think of his conversation with General Mary Thurston and the mysterious tipster whose identity they had yet to discover. Could the two incidents be connected?

He kicked the idea around his mind a little. If somebody had wanted Aymard Caron out of the way to initiate a takeover of the French-Italian Corridor, what better way to finance the operation than to use the hidden Sanchez funds? Presumably, the money would be enough to fund a mercenary crew, hideout, and other necessities.

That's a reach. But the more Kane considered the idea,

the more it made sense. It was at least worth investigating, even if he went solo while the rest of the team carried on the overseas mission. Ferrero had made the closure of the Corridor top priority. One way or another, if the separate pieces were part of the same puzzle, they'd connect. Only a matter of time.

With that, John Kane turned off the laptop and stretched out on the couch for a nap. How the rest of the crew had the energy to go bowling he had no idea. His old bones demanded rest, and he quickly dozed off into dreamland, where the sand was warm, the drinks cold, and old friends were young again.

Team Reaper HQ

"I'm beginning to wonder why you haven't said no," John Kane said.

Luis Ferrero and General Mary Thurston exchanged glances as they talked to Kane in the operations room. Ferrero shrugged. He looked at Kane. "It makes sense. I, personally, think the information from your Marine friend ties in with Caron directly."

"Why?"

"Because he had plans to head for the Bahamas. If we'd missed him in France, we'd have gone there next."

"You think he was going to look for the money himself?"

"Or join up with whoever is already there."

"Do we have any sources in the area who can confirm my friend's story?"

"Nothing has come across the usual channels," Ferrero said. "If your friend is telling the truth, I'm surprised they're operating in the open. Major players usually attract official attention."

"They could be minor players not well known," Kane said. "Anybody Don would recognize, to him, would be a big player." Kane glanced at Thurston. "Anything to add, ma'am?"

"What if Caron was working with the person who set him up?" Thurston asked.

Ferrero asked, "What do you mean?"

"The anonymous tip, remember? What if Caron was working with somebody to get the money, and that person ratted him out, so he didn't have to split?"

"Or," Kane said, "because he has another agenda like we talked about yesterday? As if he needed Caron out of the way for another reason than the money. Perhaps a takeover of the entire Corridor?"

"I'm done talking in circles," Ferrero said. "The only way to see if these items are connected is to go and look. That's for you, Reaper. We'll continue the other effort on our end, and if both items link, you'll know what to do."

Kane nodded. "I suppose I have to see if my swimsuit still fits."

"Don't look so excited," Ferrero said. "Do me a favor and take some pictures. Visiting Nassau is on my bucket list."

Kane promised to take a lot of pictures and left his chair. He stopped to say something more, a witty comeback right on the tip of his tongue but shook his head and said so long instead.

"He hasn't been himself since the team got back," Ferrero said.

"I noticed."

"I think it's more than what happened with Axe. This job is getting to him."

"Bad enough to make him want to leave?"

Ferrero said he wasn't sure. "But maybe sending him out for some sun is the best thing we can do."

"I hope you're right," Thurston said. "We can't lose him."

"He's more resilient than most. He'll be fine after a while."

Thurston said nothing more.

Somewhere over the UK

The quiet drone of the Gulfstream G550's engines didn't disturb Ceasario Crisfulli's thoughts as he watched a video on a laptop.

Only he and another, the luscious Bella Lane, occupied the private jet. There was plenty of room between them, he on one end of the right side of the plane, her further forward on the right side. They were volatile lovers. Sometimes they needed that much space, if not more, to keep from killing each other.

The laptop screen on the table in front of his tan leather chair showed combat taking place at Caron's chalet. Prior to sending the anonymous email to Team Reaper so they could do his dirty work, he'd had his crew in the ski village plant small video cameras around the chalet that would capture footage of the battle. He wished the shots had captured the faces of Team Reaper, whom he considered worthy adversaries despite having never crossed their paths previously.

He knew their mission, but none of their identities. He hoped to solve that problem someday.

The Americans never spotted the cameras hidden in the surrounding trees and elsewhere — why would they? Crisfulli felt like an invisible director of an improvised play, and his actors were the best of the best.

He had to admit, as he watched the fight, that Team Reaper was superbly coordinated, and fought easily beside the French anti-drug unit as if they'd trained together for months prior to the raid. Crisfulli knew for a fact that their alliance had had a much shorter time span. It was a testament to both adversaries. He'd never underestimated the French forces before, and certainly wouldn't now, or ever.

The fight ended, the cameras capturing only the scenery once the investigation crew had departed, long after the last bullet was fired. Crisfulli closed the laptop.

"Is it boring yet?" Bella Lane asked from the other end of the cabin. She was his computer expert, and had her own machine in front of her, the glow of the screen reflecting in her wide-frame glasses. She was a fiery redhead with a mix of Irish in her DNA and showed it when unleashing her temper. Her long locks tied back in a rebellious bun with loose strands threatening to unravel the carefully arranged hairdo.

"I could watch it ten more times and not be bored," Crisfulli said.

He wore one of his preferred white suits, not unlike the one he'd worn in Mexico when ordering the shooting of the two CIA agents after they'd completed another task seemingly for his benefit, the recovery of the lockbox containing a map noting where Jorge Sanchez had hidden his money.

"Still think they're an obstacle or something we can manipulate?"

"I'm not going to shout at you, Bella, come over here."

She rotated out of her chair, removing her glasses as she walked the length of the cabin to him. She didn't take the neighboring chair next to Crisfulli. She landed hard in his lap. He groaned sharply, trying to shift under her weight.

He smacked her left thigh. The flesh under the skirt was backed up with solid muscle. Bella Lane was no weakling. She did nothing but laugh at his slap. Her laugh sounded like wind chimes.

"You're impossible," he said.

She grinded her rear end into his lap, Crisfulli trying not to wince. She laughed again and finally settled with her arms around his neck.

"What was your question?" he asked.

"Obstacle. Yes or no?"

"They passed the test," he said. "They will follow even an anonymous email if they think it's going to give them what they're looking for, and they won't stop very long to question the source."

"And in spite of that—"

"They are very good fighters. Let's watch it again."

She slapped his hand as he reached for the laptop. She hit with the tips of her fingers, her long nails making most of the impact on his skin.

This time he laughed. As in shape as she was, she still literally "hit like a girl". Cyber espionage was Bella Lane's strong suit, not fighting.

"Enough of that video," she said.

"What have you found out on your end of the research?" he asked, trying to shift again. She had him pinned to the seat.

"They're trying to trace the email, for one thing."

"Can they?"

"Impossible. I routed it through more servers than I probably needed to. They might find one or two of those, but not the originating location."

"What else?" he asked.

"Cote will be next on the team's hit list, but they're still in El Paso. They've made no moves to continue the mission yet."

"And Caron?"

"Still in the hospital, but they'll be transferring him to Paris soon."

"How soon?"

"Tomorrow afternoon."

Crisfulli nodded. He didn't take his eyes off hers. They were dark pools of rich green, and he wanted to swim in them.

"Are we worried about Caron?" she asked.

"No. I have a feeling about what's going to happen."

"What's that?"

"My old friend will never make it to Paris."

"What makes you so sure?"

Crisfulli smiled. "I know my adversary, my dear." He smacked her behind. "Get back to work."

Bella Lane put her glasses back on and, with a grin, left his lap and returned to her computer at the other end of the cabin.

Crisfulli turned his chair to look out the port window on his right. They were still over the ocean, but their destination, Heathrow International Airport in London, was near.

Which meant their next target was close.

Close enough to feel, if he really tried.

Crisfulli thought of the lockbox secured in the Gulfstream's cargo area, along with the rest of their baggage and equipment.

The target in London was important, but not as important as the lockbox. The lockbox held the key not only to the hidden money but the revenge that Ceasario Crisfulli craved so heartily.

Crisfulli had been a member of the French-Italian Corridor and the associated syndicate in charge of the operations for over a decade. He'd run his own crew, distributed more than his share of illegal narcotics, and generally stayed out of the way of the White Wolf, that mysterious figure who relied on mystery to protect him from the machinations of law enforcement and treachery from within the ranks.

Of course, his identity was known to Crisfulli. It was known to all major plays in the Corridor, because they couldn't do business without him, nor he without them.

For two long decades, Crisfulli had played by the rules and not rocked the boat. He was everything a good cartel operator should be. He ran his crew without drama, collected money, and didn't cheat the boss.

But then the Wolf decided to rock the boat, Crisfulli's boat, specifically, taking from Crisfulli that which wasn't his. Not an object, but a person.

A woman Crisfulli had loved very much. Ariana, the tall, dark-haired beauty with the blue eyes and Crisfulli had been devoted to. If revenge was a dish best served cold, Crisfulli's meal was chilled to sub-zero temperatures. He'd been waiting for the right time, the right opportunity, the right people, and the right plan. Now, all the elements were in place. The Wolf's days were numbered.

But such plans required money. A *lot* of money.

The Sanchez treasure promised to provide that money.

And Team Reaper would contribute to the plan, albeit

unknowingly, by removing those that stood in Crisfulli's way.

The pitch of the Gulfstream's engines changed. The pilot came over the intercom and said, "We're beginning our approach to London. Fasten your lap-straps."

Bella Lane dutifully complied and resumed her work.

Crisfulli ignored the instruction.

"Where is he?" he called to Bella.

She consulted her screen. "Bascomb has not moved. Our people say they're in position." She looked over her shoulder at him. "All they're waiting for is us."

"Tell them we are almost there and shan't make them wait much longer."

The jet began to descend.

CHAPTER 6

En Route to Paris

Seven hours.

Luna Blaise glanced at her second in command, Julian Berenger. He rode shotgun while she drove and had his face in his cell phone, apparently scrolling social media.

She faced the road again. They were following the A40 out of Chamonix and away from the Alps, heading for Paris, with a plan to connect with the A6 for the rest of the journey.

"You don't look nervous at all," she said.

"Why should I be?" He didn't look at her. "Caron is locked in a cage and surrounded by four of our best shooters. What is there to be afraid of?"

Luna considered the question. She wanted to agree, but they faced plenty of danger worthy of worry. Caron had friends. Powerful friends. Friends who had yet to fall into the gunsights of Team Reaper or OCRTIS, and they very possibly might want Caron back under their protective fold.

Or they might want him dead.

And Luna Blaise wasn't sure they had enough shooters to keep either scenario from happening. She'd argued for more people, but HQ wanted Caron close to home ASAP, so they had only the bare minimum. Never mind that spies at the hospital, had there been any, probably knew all about the transfer, and HQ also hadn't set up a decoy.

Typical bureaucratic last-minute hurry-up garbage, which wouldn't be so bad if it didn't sometimes get good people killed.

She and Berenger rode in the chase car, a powerful Citroen sedan, both of them packing sidearms. Their automatic rifles were secured in the trunk.

In the ambulance ahead of them, Caron was strapped to a gurney with four shooters taking up the rest of the cramped space.

Luna's eyes not only scanned the road ahead but the side of the road too. She told Berenger to put away his phone and watch too.

"You're paranoid, boss," Berenger said. But he put his phone away and removed the pistol from his shoulder harness. He checked the chamber and tucked the gun under his left leg.

Luna Blaise thought that was a little too much, but she appreciated the effort. The hairs on her neck were standing straight. Something wasn't right. There was trouble on this road. The only question was when they'd encounter the problem.

The route certainly looked peaceful enough, mostly open space, a lot of rolling hills covered with green grass, spots of pretty flowers, homes here and there. It was a long drive into the nearest city, so it was basically country living, the kind of lifestyle Luna Blaise wished she could lead, but her work demanded full-time living in the city.

Presently the A40 connected to the A6, and they made the transition without a problem. Driving in the country meant little to no traffic. They'd hit delays on the approach to Paris for sure, though.

Berenger said, "I'm surprised you and Kane didn't get a little friendlier."

They passed under the Route de Polliat overcrossing.

"What do you mean?" she asked.

"We could all tell there was a little more going on than mission planning."

"There was nothing like that!"

"Well, maybe you didn't notice. But he looked like he wanted a date."

"If that's true," she said, feeling herself loosening up, "maybe next time he passes through he'll have the guts to ask for one."

Those were her last words.

"Almost in range," said the mercenary with the code name of Voltaire.

Adalene Severin thought the code name was silly, but there was no doubt that "Voltaire" and his merc crew were one of the best, had served the Corridor well, and were available on short notice.

Voltaire sighted through the scope of a Barrett .50-caliber rifle with the stock tucked tightly into his right shoulder, one eye closed, full focus through the optic mounted on top of the rifle.

Adalene Severin very rarely killed anybody these days.

Instead, she directed the shooters who did the real killing while she lined up the elements necessary for the assassination to happen without a hitch.

And Voltaire didn't miss.

Adalene used binoculars to track the ambulance and the Citroen sedan trailing behind. They were well away from the road, unlike the rest of Voltaire's crew, who would make the direct assault. Their job was to take out the leadership in the sedan. It was the perfect day to hang out in a grassy field; in fact, lay in the grass, the sun shining overhead and birds chirping to complete the tranquility.

In other words, it was also a nice day to kill a bunch of federal cops. There was hardly any other traffic on the A6 at this hour. They had to work fast if they wanted such conditions to remain.

Adalene counted only two people in the sedan, a female driving, and a male in the passenger seat. Her intel said the woman would be Luna Blaise, the new chief of OCRTIS. This would be a feather in the cap for sure. OCRTIS was still reeling from the arrest and prosecution of their previous chief. Adding a dead one to the misery would be a terrific achievement.

Adalene thought it was sad that she could never brag about such achievements. One didn't necessarily put their latest kills on the refrigerator, after all.

"Got 'em," Voltaire said.

"Take the shot."

The Barrett boomed. The shot was a signal to the rest of his crew, closer to the road, to spring into action. Adalene kept the sedan in focus as the .50-cal bullet crashed through the windshield, creating a hole big enough to toss a watermelon, taking off the driver's head in less time than it took to blink. The passenger's mouth opened as he screamed, the car drifting off the road, catching in a ditch, and overturning multiple times before coming to rest on its roof in a grass field.

She switched her attention to the ambulance, shifting her body to the right to watch the mercenary crew attack.

A volley of fully automatic gunfire struck the front of the ambulance, tearing the two wheels to shreds. The ambulance slammed forward on steel rims, sparks rising, the screech reaching even Adalene's ears despite the distance. Voltaire fired again, a kill-shot through the hood and into the engine that stopped the vehicle in its tracks.

Driver and passenger attempted to get out with their own weapons, but the 4-man merc crew jumped from roadside cover and opened fire again. Both men dropped, riddled with lead. By the time the rear doors of the ambulance opened, and the heavily armed and black-clad OCRTIS operatives joined the fray, they were too late. The mercs were already there, attacking with rifle butts and pistols. The gunfire crackled, echoing into the distance; the screams of the OCRTIS troops weren't as audible, but Adalene licked her lips as she imagined the sounds.

Maybe one picture on the refrigerator won't hurt.

The merc crew jumped into the vehicle. Voltaire used a hand-held radio to call the extraction vehicle, which quickly pulled onto the road from a mile away and raced to the attack site. By the time the merc crew hauled a still-shackled and obviously sedated and bandaged Aymard Caron out of the ambulance, the Volkswagen Amarok pick-up truck was in position. The crew loaded Caron into the rear of the cabin, jumped in, and the truck made a sharp U-turn before speeding off into the distance.

"Well," Voltaire said, finally turning his eyes to Adalene instead of his rifle scope. "Shall we take a walk?"

To the Land Rover parked a quarter mile away.

"Sure." Adalene smiled and started to stand up.

They'd rendezvous with the merc crew, and Caron, at a private airstrip about a day's drive away. Their Land Rover was waiting where they left it, near a cluster of trees, and Adalene let Voltaire take the driver's seat.

Once aboard the private jet, they'd get Caron cleaned up and talking before bringing him to face the White Wolf, and the questions about who betrayed him, and why.

London

Crisfulli checked his watch as the driver of the Mercedes kept up with traffic.

Bella Lane slapped his wrist.

"Stop looking at your watch."

"Hit me again, and I'll break your hand."

"Promise?"

He laughed. He put both hands in his lap. The back seat of the Mercedes was quite comfortable, and the driver very knowledgeable of London streets. He had managed to avoid a couple of long delays so far, and the current flow pleased Crisfulli greatly. He looked ahead. The passing scenery meant nothing to him. He wasn't in London to see the sights. He was in London to kidnap a man named Leland Bascomb and take him to Nassau.

Crisfulli's "treasure hunt" would have far fewer problems with the Bascomb alongside him.

Too bad he had to be snatched against his will, and his family threatened, to make sure he complied.

But Leland Bascomb didn't know that yet.

"How long until the lecture is over?"

"He will be speaking for another forty-five minutes," Bella Lane said. "We have plenty of time."

Crisfulli slouched in his seat. His formerly perfectly pressed white suit was starting to show wrinkles, especially the pants and jacket. His shirt was holding up much better.

"Sitting like that is bad for your back," Bella Lane said.

"Wanna know what's good for my back?"

She patted his leg. "The driver is listening, dear. Control yourself."

Crisfulli grinned. The driver glanced back in his rearview but made no comment. Crisfulli didn't know the man's name. He didn't know half the names of the mercenary crew Bella had engaged; he didn't need to know. All he needed from them was the advertised efficiency. He needed them to do their job and keep their mouths shut.

Queen Mary University of London
School of Biological and Chemical Sciences

Leland Bascomb talked about marine biology the way a parent talked about their first child, full of pride, excitement, a little fear of the mystery ahead, but also ready to tackle the obstacles.

He hoped to pass that enthusiasm to his students.

The best way to do that, Bascomb thought, was to show them recent ocean discoveries that might excite them, and explain that there was plenty more to find, that old timers like him had done their bit, and now it was time for them to step aside and let the next generation take up the torch.

"What do you see here?" he asked his class, his voice

loud and contained within the classroom. It was a circular room with stadium-type diagonal seating, and the small group of students clustered near the front row watched Bascomb's latest large-screen video presentation with rapt attention.

One student said, "A sunny beach."

"Where?"

"Nowhere in London."

The students laughed.

Bascomb laughed too. The key to surviving the boring parts of marine biology, and there were enough to put anybody to sleep on the nights where one goes to bed and promptly starts thinking about the wreck they've made of their life and how it's probably too late to change anything, was to keep a sense of humor.

"What you're looking at," Bascomb said, "is the Under-water Waterfall."

The video didn't appear to lie. The screen showed water as crystal-clear as anyone in the room had ever seen ocean water, the V of a land mass in the center. The activity in the V was where the camera focused, and it appeared that water was falling into the ocean from atop the surface.

He glanced at his students. Some wore deep frowns.

"How can water fall underwater, you ask? Any ideas?"

A woman asked, "It's a pool?"

"Yes, and no," Bascomb said.

No other students offered a suggestion.

Bascomb paused the video.

"This is one of those once-in-a-lifetime finds, and it was discovered recently," he explained. "What we have here is Mauritius Island, in the Indian Ocean. That V right there marks a spot where both sand and silt are washing into the ocean and it creates the effect of a surface waterfall. Amazing, isn't it?"

The students agreed it was amazing.

Bascomb turned off the video and perched on the edge of his desk. He addressed his students with a grin.

"Think of what *you* will find in the coming years."

Somebody scoffed.

"Who disagrees?"

The scoffing student said, "There isn't anything left to find. Guys like you and Cousteau have seen it all."

"Then why are you in this class, Mr. Sanderson?"

"To learn how to protect the environment. It's the only thing left for us to do."

"Not quite," Bascomb said. "What if I told you that people like me and Cousteau have barely scratched the surface of what's in the ocean? Sights like this" — he gestured to the blank video screen— "and so much more. Did you know that 80-percent of the ocean is unmapped? Nobody has ever been to those areas, and I'm not talking about deep, deep ocean exploring, Mr. James Cameron's feat notwithstanding. By the time we can go into the darkest of the dark ocean places, I'll be long gone. It will be up to you to see the things I could only dream about."

Bascomb paused as the students soaked in the information.

"What do you think now, Mr. Sanderson? Protecting the ocean is noble, no question, but it's not all you're limited to."

"I'll have to do more reading," Sanderson said.

"Much, much more reading! Lots more reading! Exploring starts with reading, everything you can, about where you want to go. And even then, you never learn enough. By the time you get where you're going, you might as well not have bothered. Like everything else in life."

The students laughed.

"That's all the time we have for today," Bascomb said. "See you later in the week." The students began to gather their belongings. "Read chapter twelve of the textbook, please," Bascomb called out, most of the students halfway to the exit. Most of them would read the text, though. The rest would sit quietly while they caught up with the discussion.

Bascomb left the corner of his desk and sat down to sort papers and fill his briefcase with tests that required grading. This particular class met three days a week, and he needed to get the tests graded by the next meeting, and back in the hands of his students, so they could do whatever they did with returned tests. Used them to make paper airplanes? He was still new to teaching, and now had an idea why some of his colleagues simply posted grades on a bulletin board outside the classroom. He hated to admit that his own ocean exploring days had long ago come to an end, but that was a fact of life. Now he wanted to spend the rest of his life sharing his enthusiasm with the future explorers of the world. It wasn't a bad trade-off.

He'd certainly had his share of glory. Cousteau was the household name, but Bascomb had more than made his mark in the arena too.

His lower back hurt as he stood up from his chair. He cursed. Sitting on the edge of the deck always did that, sent a stabbing pain through his lower back, probably to remind him that he wasn't a young spit anymore. Didn't his body communicate that in other ways? He decided he'd had enough of such messages, but how to tell his joints to behave?

He grabbed his briefcase and started up the steps to the

exit. It was still nice out, without being painfully hot. Summers in London were always rough, but today Mother Nature had decided to take it easy on the Londoners.

He walked briskly to the parking lot where his BMW 7-Series waited. His teaching salary didn't pay for the car; his undersea adventures and assorted television specials, book deals, and speaking engagements fixed his income so that the teaching salary was gravy. He had more money than he'd need; his two sons would certainly benefit when he and his wife were gone.

Bascomb opened the trunk and chucked his briefcase inside.

Closing the lid, he made his way to the driver's door, and stopped at the sight of a curvaceous woman in a green dress, with captivating green eyes behind wide-framed glasses, her red hair tied back, who stood near the front wing of the car.

"May I help you?"

"No," the woman said.

Bascomb frowned, but as he tried to respond, what felt like ten thousand needles pierced his skin through the fabric of his tweed blazer and cotton shirt. If he thought sitting on the edge of a desk made his back hurt, this new pain was ten times that feeling. And then everything went black.

Leland Bascomb felt dizzy.

He came to in the back of a speeding Mercedes, jammed into the back seat between the redheaded woman and a man in a white suit.

The man said, "We should have brought a van. I had no idea it would be so hard stuffing you into the back seat."

Bascomb looked at his hands. They were in his lap but shackled with handcuffs.

He wanted to ask what was the meaning of this, who are you, what is happening, but while the words formed in his mind, his mouth refused to form them audibly.

"Relax," the man in white said. He produced a smartphone from his inside jacket pocket and held it out for Bascomb to see.

A picture on the screen showed his wife, gagged, and bound to a chair, her eyes wide with fear.

"You will cooperate, and everything will be okay. Understand?"

Bascomb managed a nod.

"My name is Ceasario Crisfulli. You've never heard of me. We are going to Nassau because we need to look for treasure under the sea, and your presence in my expedition will make certain officials very happy to comply with my requests. You're a famous explorer, after all. This will be your great comeback project. You'll be famous again!" Crisfulli laughed.

Bascomb found no humor in the situation.

"We used a Taser on you," Crisfulli continued. "You probably feel rotten. The effects will wear off soon. Remember to keep cool. My people will stay with Evelyn during the project, and I don't expect to need you more than a couple of days."

Bascomb's face froze in fear.

"I promise you won't be hurt," Crisfulli said. "I have killed many men, but nobody who didn't deserve it, okay?"

Bascomb faced forward. He felt a vice gripping his chest, a pit in his stomach. *Evelyn!* His wife of 40 years. Where were his sons?

As if reading his mind, Crisfulli said, "Your sons remain

under surveillance. They won't be harmed if you cooperate. Keep that in mind. The only thing you face is trouble with the university for disappearing."

Bascomb breathed heavily.

"Won't be long," Crisfulli said, and then went quiet.

Bascomb's pulse pounded in his head. The steel hand-cuffs rattled as his hands shook.

CHAPTER 7

El Paso International Airport.
El Paso, TX

"Ain't you lucky," Brick said.

The 6'3" team medic drove John Kane to the airport in his personal vehicle, a Cadillac Escalade. It was one of the few vehicles, Brick liked to joke, where the roof was high enough that he didn't bang his bald head every time he drove over a bump.

Kane sat in the passenger seat with his carry on tote bag at his feet. He didn't want to admit it to Brick, but he did feel lucky. Lucky to get away from HQ and the team for a short time, even if the trip turned into a mission. He simply needed to get lost for a while and re-center himself.

His single suitcase sat on the back seat. It was a "special" suitcase with built-in compartments for various tools of the trade. In the X-ray proof compartment attached to the bottom of the case, Kane had placed his SIG-Sauer M17 autoloader, two boxes of ammunition, and a set of magazines. Any heavier hardware required would have to be picked up on-site or delivered. For all he knew, Don Mateo already had a stash of fully loaded automatic rifles waiting for hard use.

"This is not a vacation," Kane said.

"Nuts. You're saying that so we don't rag on you too much."

"It may turn into a mission very quickly."

"We already got a mission. Waiting for the brass to send us out again. What's this one got to do with that one?"

"What if I told you they think these two threads are connected?"

"Are they?"

"Could be."

"That's your excuse for going on vacation."

Kane laughed.

"Who is the guy you're visiting that says he can spot a cartel dude so easily?"

Kane made a quick rundown of Don Mateo's credentials, including his current occupation as "consultant" and troubleshooter. Brick pressed his lips together, nodding.

"Well, I'm convinced," said the big man.

"Good, because I'm done trying to prove the case," Kane said. "The Sanchez money may be a legend, but I don't think we'd see this kind of activity in one area if it were a complete hoax."

"Grab a few bucks for me," Brick said. "I want a back tattoo."

"Your arms aren't enough?"

Brick's bulging forearms sported tattoos on either side, decorative artwork that wasn't Kane's cup of tea. He preferred to keep his own tattoo, the Grim Reaper, on his back, where only he knew where it was, like a good luck charm. He could, at least, appreciate the attention to detail in Brick's ink. The tattoo artist who'd put the images there knew his craft well indeed.

"Naw, man, gotta have a dragon on my back."

"What would you do if you found all that money yourself?"

Brick shrugged. "Buy a new car?"

"That's it?"

"Buy two? What would you do?"

Kane opened his mouth to reply, then had to admit he had no idea. A new car sounded like a fine solution with the rest left in the bank. He'd never have to work again.

Or fight again.

He could let the young bucks on their way up in the ranks take over the everlasting war.

Maybe he really had reached his limit, whatever that limit was.

A visit with Don and Katie Mateo might be what the doctor ordered. Nassau was about as far away from Texas and Team Reaper as he could get without putting on a parka and heading for the Aleutians.

Which didn't sound bad, either.

Brick presently steered the Cadillac to the curbside at the departure terminal of El Paso International. The departure terminal was jammed with cars, passengers hauling luggage, and airport police blowing whistles. Typical airport chaos. Kane jumped out, grabbed his suitcase from the back seat, and turned to find Brick coming around the front of the car.

"Good luck and call us when you need us."

The pair shook hands, Brick slapping Kane on the right arm. Kane grunted from the blow. "Brick" was an appropriate name.

"Don't play poker with a woman named Thelma," Brick said, on his way back to the driver's side.

"What the heck does that mean?" Kane called out.

"Advice my father gave me. Saved my life once."

And with that, Brick drove off.

Kane headed into the terminal. As the automatic doors shut behind him, quieting some of the noise from outside, he crossed the polished tiles to the check-in desk and squared away his boarding pass. Passing through security after a thirty-minute wait, he grabbed a Coke and found his gate, sitting down to kill the remaining hour before his flight.

Thoughts swirled like a hurricane in his mind. Too many to sort out. Too many he didn't want to dwell on or admit existed. Too much thinking can do a lot of damage to a man who felt vulnerable, and Kane had to admit that's exactly how he felt. They might have lost Burton in France; the tourists killed in the cartel crossfire south of El Paso might have lived if Team Reaper had been there.

Kane drank some Coke. He had to stop the cycle. He had to focus on the days ahead, and a reunion with an old friend.

Regardless of how the Nassau visit turned out, Kane hoped the sun and surf would help clear his head and help him focus on looming battles.

Because the war had no end.

Team Reaper HQ

Cara Billings didn't understand the delay.

Why weren't they in France or Italy tearing up the

Corridor like they'd planned? Why had Axe's capture apparently thrown a monkey wrench into the works? Who cared who was behind the stupid email. They'd find out soon enough if they continued shooting bad guys. And if they shot enough of them, the source of the email wouldn't matter anymore anyway.

She didn't join Team Reaper to sit around and paint her fingernails. They were currently pink, but still close-cropped because long nails and machine guns didn't mix.

In the bedroom at her apartment, she zipped her jeans and sat on the bed long enough to tie a pair of running shoes, then grabbed purse, keys, and her cell phone and went out to her car. She'd checked on her son the previous evening, per her usual routine, and was relieved to know he was still doing well and hanging in there despite being away from her. As long as she worked for Team Reaper, it was too dangerous for Jimmy to be anywhere else. They made plans to see each other in the coming months; hopefully as soon as the French-Italian mission was over. If it ever finished.

She checked in at HQ. Thurston had nothing to report other than Sam Swift, the red-haired hacker, might have some information for them soon.

Cara collected her pistol from the ready room and a pair of earmuffs from the office outside the warehouse shooting range and joined the rest of the team inside. Arenas, Brick, and Burton lined shooting stalls, firing pistols at stationary paper targets down the line.

Burton practiced rapid-fire drills. Two quick rounds to the chest, one to the head. The classic Mozambique drill, developed by accident during Mozambican War for Independence, and later incorporated into the curriculum of combat instructors throughout the world. Cara didn't like the technique. The third shot, aimed at the head, more than likely missed most of the time during the heat of combat. If two rounds to the chest couldn't stop a threat, Cara preferred to aim lower, at the beltline, which was the same width as the torso, and fire another pair of rounds, with the goal of destroying an enemy's hip area. Break the hips, the chassis of the human body, and the bad guy can't stay upright no matter how ineffective the chest shots might have been. Once he was on the ground, the headshot was much easier.

But Burton looked good. He needed a haircut. The mop on his head was getting a little unruly, especially around the ears. Otherwise, he appeared as his usual, obnoxious self, and Cara wouldn't have it any other way.

Axe emptied his magazine with a final trio of rounds and removed the empty mag from the grip. Cara slapped him on the back. "How you feeling?" she asked, shouting over the gunfire from the other stalls.

"Good as new!"

Axe pressed a button on the stall wall to his left and brought the target toward him. The track in the ceiling rumbled as the chain brought the target to him.

What had started as a black silhouette was still black, mostly. It was black with a lot of tiny holes all over the paper.

"Lots of holes in that target of yours!"

"Especially the head!" He laughed.

"You know I don't like headshots. You're taking a big chance hoping for that kind of hit!"

"Hey, John Wick always makes his headshots!"

"John Wick is the figment of somebody's imagination!"

Axe laughed. "Look who's talking!"

Cara shook her head and retreated to the wall of shelves in the rear of the range, where she found a selection of ammunition. Most of the hollow-point defensive loads had been taken, and she cast a frown at the men behind her. That meant she was left with practice ammo—full-metal jacket stuff. Not that the ammo was bad, but she preferred to practice with what she'd actually use in the field. Oh, well. A bad day at the range is better than a good day anywhere else. She picked out a box of Federal full metal jacket and took the shooting stall next to Axe, who was reloading his magazines. The team was going out of their skulls waiting for the next move against the French-Italian Corridor; a little trigger therapy seemed appropriate.

She didn't want to think about Reaper's little excursion to the land of sun and surf. Sometimes he really pissed her off. This was one of those times.

A paper target already hung from the automatic rail at the end of Cara's stall. She was about to load her mags and start shooting when red lights flashed, and the range master's voice echoed over the speaker:

"Cease-fire."

The crew stopped shooting, looking back through the dusty window in the back of the range to the office.

"General Thurston wants you all to report immediately," the range master said. He hung up his microphone.

"Well crap," Brick said, removing his earmuffs. "I was halfway from shooting a perfect smiley face."

"We've been busy," Thurston said as Team Reaper, minus Kane, filtered into the operations room and sat around the conference table. There was a flow chart with various names on the wide screen behind her.

Brick said, "That makes some of us."

Thurston raised an eyebrow at Reaper's big man but made no comment. She addressed the table.

Cara looked at Thurston's face. There were more lines than usual, and her light makeup didn't cover the fact that there were dark circles under her eyes. She looked tired. Cara wondered when she'd slept last, and suddenly decided simply being bored wasn't so bad.

And it made her wonder exactly what the HQ crew had discovered.

"Our people in France are dead," Thurston began.

Blood drained from Cara's face. Her teammates were equally stunned.

"It happened a few hours ago, while Luna Blaise, Julian Berenger, and a tactical team were transporting Caron back to Paris."

"What happened?" Cara asked.

"Ambush."

"Is Caron dead?"

"There was no sign of Caron at the ambush site," Thurston said. "He was taken out of the ambulance. We assume he's still alive, whereabouts unknown."

"Are we recalling Kane from Nassau?"

"No, because what he's doing there might tie in with our current project."

"How?"

"Not sure how. Yet. Speculation."

"What *are* we sure of?" Cara asked, her voice rising. She'd liked Blaise and her crew. She felt like a dozen knives had been driven into her chest.

"Slick has been up all night," Thurston said, referred to red-headed hacker Sam Swift by his nickname, "and he put together this flow chart of the French-Italian Corridor." She turned to face the screen. "As you know, we blank at the very top for the White Wolf. Down below, you see Caron's name. Below that, set off to the left and right, is Desire Cote and Ceasario Crisfulli."

"We know this, ma'am," Arenas said.

"This ties in with that mysterious email," Thurston said. "Either one of these two may have arranged that anonymous tip that told you where to find Axe."

"Any talking in the usual circles?" Cara asked.

"We haven't picked up any chatter," Thurston said. "Tracing the email is useless. It bounced all over the world before it reached you at the ski village."

"Because somebody wanted the trail hidden," Brick said. "I think you're right, ma'am. One of those two, or maybe somebody else, is trying to kill their way to the big chair."

"And that treasure in Nassau might be the fuel for the operations," Arenas said.

"And," Thurston added, "we think they're using us to do most of the dirty work."

Cara looked around, not agreeing or disagreeing. They were probably right, she decided. It was too much of a coincidence to have all these threads appearing at the same time. She turned her attention back to Thurston.

"What's the plan, ma'am?"

"Gather information. We need to know if we're right. If Crisfulli or Cote or another individual is making a power play, we need to stop them. If they can lead us to the top dog so we can smash the syndicate for good, even better. As long as Aymard Caron remains alive, our work so far has been for nothing. I'm not in the habit of wasting time."

"The next question is," Cara said, "who's going to tell Kane about Luna Blaise?"

Not a soul answered.

. . .

Nassau
    The Bahamas

John Kane whistled as the passenger jet deposited passengers at the arrival terminal of Lynden Pindling International Airport. The airport wasn't as large as others he was familiar with in the States or around the world, but the small airport had the best view of all of them, crystal clear ocean water and the sunniest blue sky Kane had seen in forever. The architects of the terminal knew what they were doing when they put the arrival section in perfect view of the ocean and made sure one side of the building was all glass.

Clear glass, too. A uniformed maintenance crew not far from Kane was busily wiping the pane up one side and down the other to keep the view pristine.

At least until people actually wandered outside.

That was the whole point of visiting Nassau, after all.

Kane went down an escalator to baggage claim where the carousels were already spinning with bags, and tourists were jammed elbow-to-elbow. A sign held by a man that read "Corporal Kane" caught Reaper One's attention, and he gritted his teeth as he went over and pretended to punch Don Mateo in the gut.

"That's *Gunny* to you," Kane said.

Mateo laughed and lowered the sign, heartily shaking Kane's hand.

"Where's Katie?"

"Still at the hotel," Mateo said. "She wanted to give us some guy time."

"I haven't seen her since the wedding."

It took another twenty minutes for Kane to collect his suitcase and fight his way through the crowd to the outside, where the crisp air and sunshine invigorated him right away.

"You don't know how important this visit is, Don," he said.

Mateo laughed. "It's all over your face."

"It's been tough, man."

They crossed a walkway through vehicle arrival traffic to the parking lot, where Mateo unlocked the doors to a four-door gray BMW 330i sedan.

"Still prefer poor people cars?" Kane asked.

"Keep that up, and you're walking."

Mateo popped the trunk, and Kane stowed his suitcase and carry on and closed the lid gently, the trunk closing on its own as a hydraulic motor performed to action. The trunk lock clicked quietly. He joined Mateo inside the car.

"These seats are like my couch."

Mateo started the car. The engine offered a throaty rumble.

"Yeah, that's why I like 'em."

"Dashboard looks like a video game, though. How do you tell what's what?"

"It's a sixth sense BMW drivers have. You wouldn't know."

Kane laughed. It felt good to laugh and spend time with Don again.

"It's been too long, pal," Kane said.

Mateo agreed and drove out of the parking lot.

"See any boogeymen lately?" Kane asked once Mateo had merged with traffic.

"They're all over the place," Mateo said. "Although I

must admit, they've been laying low around the hotel. There was a flurry of activity over the last few days, but now they've settled down."

"What kind of activity?"

"Arrivals mostly. A few hushed meetings around the pool, stuff like that. Now they're hanging out. We have pictures."

"Really?"

"Katie's former Air Force intelligence, remember? She knows how to snap a pic and not be seen."

"You sound more excited about the caper than the vacation."

"You know what? You're right. This has been more exciting than laying around the beach all day. We threw out our original itinerary a long time ago."

Mateo followed John F. Kennedy Drive after leaving the airport. Kane shook his head. Every spot in the world seemed to have a road or building or school named after the late US president. He'd wished he'd been alive to see the real impact the man had made on the country and the world. Reading history books and watching old news and documentary footage didn't truly give the same feel as real life.

The sky above was clear, and Kane wished the 330i had a ragtop to fully appreciate and take in the view. Kane powered down the window and leaned out a little, the wind whipping at his forehead. A few scattered clouds, the sky a deeper blue than Kane remembered seeing in Texas.

The ocean was off Mateo's side of the car, but Kane saw no sign of the water. Buildings and other structures lining the coast blocked the view entirely. Kane sighed. He was happy Nassau had attracted so many people with its beauty but saddened to see such beauty marred by the usual signs of too many people in too small a space.

"Nice, huh?" Mateo asked. "We could retire here."

"And do what?"

"We'll open a bait shop. Everybody who owns a bait and tackle shop makes millions off the tourists."

"Easy Street, here we come."

"It's never easy, Johnny."

"True enough," Kane said. "But it's really tempting. I remember fishing with my pop. Used to catch trout and mom cooked it just right."

Mateo's voice sounded grim. "I think we have a tail."

Kane's mind went into tactical mode.

No more trips down memory lane, for now.

"Tail as in whale?" he asked.

"No, tail as in the same black Mercedes has been behind us since we left the airport."

Kane twisted in his seat to look out the back window. He spotted the black Mercedes as the driver took cover behind a truck. *Naughty naughty.*

Kane faced forward again. "Welcome wagon?"

"I think the fun might be over," Mateo said. "If they're following me, you can bet they know we've been watching them."

"At least you know you haven't been hallucinating. Think Katie's okay?"

Mateo laughed. "Katie's fine, trust me. You packing?"

"Pistol in the trunk."

"Why don't we—"

"Now's not the time for a gunfight," Kane said. "Let's take solace in the fact that you're right, something's going on around here, you've been compromised, and we're about to have an old-fashioned hammer party."

Mateo let out a whoop. "Who says we're too young for the old days?"

Kane laughed again. "This weather is making me feel 18 all over again. Full of piss and vinegar. The exact *opposite* of how I've felt lately, all the vinegar's gone." *I sound like an old man. Get your head back in the game!*

"We're almost to the hotel."

"Good, I could use a drink."

CHAPTER 8

"Luna Blaise and her number two were killed while transporting Caron to Paris," General Thurston said. "So were four members of her strike force."

John Kane gripped his cell so tightly he almost crushed the case. "And Caron?"

"Unaccounted for, presumed alive."

Kane ended the call as Thurston resumed talking. He tossed the phone on the bed. He wasn't in the mood for her right now. The phone rang again, but he ignored it. Let her talk all she wanted into his voice mail.

Kane put his hands on his hips and glanced around the well-appointed room. Too bad the impression had been ruined. He faced the patio windows that overlooked the ocean, and suddenly didn't care any longer.

He had liked Luna Blaise; probably more than he wanted to admit, but romantic entanglements in the middle of a mission was a one-way ticket to disaster. He hadn't figured out what he might do once the mission ended. The capture of Axe put a wrench into the whole machine. And now it looked as if getting Axe back alive was the only successful part of the mission in France.

Should he call Thurston and tell her he was coming home? He shook his head. He had a job to do in Nassau, and the tail who'd followed them from the airport proved Mateo wasn't simply looking for attention and a reason to call an old battle buddy. There was something happening in Nassau. It might be connected to France. Kane wanted to find out. Worst case, it wasn't, and he'd shut down cartel activity on this end while the rest of the crew handled Europe. He'd link up with them once again soon enough.

Good-bye, Luna. We'll get 'em.

But Kane had been around long enough to know that vengeance never healed the loss of a friend or colleague. It was another useless gesture, like so many others in his world, but some gestures had to be made.

Just because.

And he was okay with that.

If Caron has visions of getting away, he's sorely mistaken.

Kane turned back to the bed where his suitcase lay, unzipped the top and began unpacking his clothes. He saved his pistol for last, and carefully loaded each magazine before stowing the weapon in his shoulder holster and shrugging into the rig. He covered the weapon and spare ammo with a jacket. He might be the only one in Nassau not dressed for the weather, but he didn't care. Each bullet had a name on it. Kane intended to deliver each package accurately, and without hesitation.

Now Kane really needed a drink.

Don Mateo noticed right away the look on his face as he

approached the table where Don and his wife sat. Mateo stood up, pulling back the extra chair.

"You okay?"

"Got some bad news."

Kane dropped into the seat and explained the phone call, then realized Katie Mateo was staring at him.

"Forgive me, Katie," he said, getting up to go around for a hug.

"I understand," she said.

"Haven't seen you since the wedding, you look great."

"Apparently I stand out more than I thought."

Kane forced a smile. He really needed to work his facial muscles to make a smile, but he made it, and then sat down again.

"I ordered mojitos," Mateo said.

"That's fine," Kane said.

"We'll get 'em, buddy," Mateo said. "Every single one of them."

Kane nodded. He was about to say more when the waiter arrived with the tray of mojitos.

When the waiter departed, Mateo raised his glass.

"To old friends and new adventures."

"Hear, hear," Katie said.

Kane said nothing.

They clinked glasses. Kane swallowed a sip of the drink and let the alcohol rush through him. The mixture was potent. A few more sips and he'd feel much better than when he'd come downstairs.

They were staying at the Melia Nassau Beach All-Inclusive Resort, and Kane wondered why they'd have to venture outside the walls. The hotel had several bars and restaurants to enjoy, and unless there was something spectacular down the street or whatever, he didn't mind the idea of dining at the hotel.

From the wide patio area containing not only two large pools on either end but several more bars under canopies, they had a terrific view of the ocean, the water so clear Kane could see the sand below the water's surface, even with all the bodies and boats already in the water.

Don Mateo said, "I know you're probably not in the mood now—"

"I am," Kane said.

"Well, look at your nine o'clock."

Kane glanced left as he sipped his drink and spotted a white man with a decent tan and black hair, wearing a pair of shorts and no shirt. His barrel-chest blended in with any number of similarly bodied men on the patio, and his face meant nothing to Kane. The obvious scars on his upper body suggested he was either very clumsy or a combat veteran.

Kane said, "Don't know him. How do you know he's with a cartel?"

Katie already had her cell phone out, using her thumb to scroll through pictures. "Because I caught him with this guy." She handed Kane the phone, and he examined the face on the screen.

She had zoomed in so Kane could have a better look at the man, and there was no doubting his identity. Kane used his thumb and index finger to zoom out and caught the second man at the table, Barrel Chest. Both were in a heated discussion.

Kane handed Katie back her phone.

"Yup," Kane said, "him I recognize. "Mr. Carlos Lorenzo."

"I crossed his path in Colombia," Mateo said. "I'll never forget that face. Had him in my sights once but missed."

"Shame," Kane said

"Which cartel is he with now?" Mateo asked.

"He's a bit player in something called the French-Italian Corridor," Kane said. "In other words, his presence here ties up my current case with what's happening with this treasure hunt." *That was fast. And almost too easy.* But Kane knew when to take "yes" for an answer. Now to gather all the remaining pieces and try to make sense of the puzzle. He grinned at Katie. "Nice picture, Chair Force."

She smiled. "We're not as lazy as we look."

"What else do you have on him?"

"He likes betting on the horses," Katie said. "There's a track not too far from here. He goes there almost every afternoon."

"Bets heavy?"

"Not always," she said. "Maybe once or twice a day. The rest of the time he sits and watches. It's like he'd rather see the races than the ocean."

Kane shrugged. Everybody enjoyed a vacation in their own way. He swallowed more of the mojito. Yup, he was starting to feel perfectly fine.

"I need to run those pictures past my boss if she's still talking to me."

"What did you do?" Mateo asked.

"Hung up on her."

"That's all?"

"Yup."

"You're getting soft in your old age, Reaper."

Kane smiled again, but this time, he didn't have to force his mouth to move.

. . .

Paris

"I'm not dead," Aymard Caron said.

"You're lucky."

Caron didn't realize he wasn't alone in the room. The first thing he noticed was no windows, only bright fluorescent lights reflecting off white walls. He was in a bed, a normal hospital bed, with bars raised on either side. Then he noticed he was handcuffed to the raised rails.

He turned his head to the right and looked at the woman in the corner. She sat in a leather chair, her legs crossed, a fashion magazine in her lap, purse on the floor beside the chair.

"You," he said.

"Me," said Adalene Severin.

"Where am I?"

"Above ground."

"I thought they'd done me in."

"They might have, but you know French doctors. They're very good at saving people who still have questions to answer."

Caron tried to lift his arms, but the cuffs prevented him from moving more than a fraction. "And the meaning of the shackles?"

"We're not sure which side you're on, love."

"He's here, isn't he?"

"You might be in one of his many domiciles," Adalene said.

Caron glanced at his clothing. He was still in the hospital gown, but there were spots of red on the fabric.

"It's not your blood," Adalene explained. "You came through the rough-and-tumble stuff very well, albeit you were obviously sedated. Your stitching held up, and if you stay in bed, you should heal nicely."

"Unless?"

"Unless it turns out you're on the wrong side, Aymard." She picked up her magazine again. "I'm only here to babysit you until he arrives."

"When?"

"Soon enough. Lay there and stare at the ceiling for a while."

"You couldn't bring a TV in here?"

"You're lucky you got away with your life," Adalene said. She put her face in the magazine. "Now hush. I'm reading about new purses."

The door opened so quietly neither Caron nor Adalene Severin heard it swing.

They heard the heavy footsteps of the person entering, though.

Adalene slowly rose from her chair, placing the fashion magazine face down on the cushion. She rushed for no man. When she straightened, Jean-Bernard Page stood in the room about two feet away from Caron's bed.

Page wasn't a big man, resembling an older Alfred Hitchcock complete with a black suit, white shirt, black tie. He looked harmless, but that was the point. Nobody realized, on the few occasions where he actually left his home, that he was the leader of the biggest narco-trafficking outfit in Western Europe. Nobody knew that he was the White Wolf.

His humble beginnings in the Union Corse paled in comparison to his position now. Some said he was God-like, but even he wasn't willing to go *that* far. He wielded the kind of power most men only dreamed of yet held that power in check because using it meant the possibility of exposure. He planned to die in bed, comfortable, not rotting in a jail cell. He had to maintain the discipline necessary to reach that goal.

He told Adalene to sit down again. She did.

The old man turned to the bed.

"Hello, Aymard," Page said. He spoke clearly, and with authority. He liked to say that his surname meant "servant" and that selling narcotics "served" the greater population that needed such narcotics in order to survive. The fact that his drugs brought high crime, misery, death, along with obscene profits to his coffers, didn't concern him.

"Monsieur Page," Caron said. "Why am I handcuffed to this bed? You know me."

"Do we really, Aymard?" Page slowly approached the bed. "Do we?"

Caron tightened his fists. "I'd like somebody to explain what's going on."

"We would too, Aymard."

"Considering I don't know anything, perhaps—"

"What do you know?"

"I know," Caron said, "that I was targeted by the Americans and OCRTIS. I *know* I captured one of the Americans and attempted to use him as a bargaining chip, but then I *know* somebody told where he was hidden, and that led to a raid on my beautiful chalet."

Page grunted.

"That's all I *know*," Caron said.

"I don't think you're funny."

"I don't think you're looking past your nose," Caron said, adding: "Sir."

Adalene reached for her purse. "Shall I kill him?"

Page lifted his right hand and made a "down" gesture.

"What's going on in Nassau?" Page asked Caron.

"What?"

"I won't repeat myself, Aymard."

Caron sighed. "Side project. Somebody thinks they found several *million* US dollars buried by one of the Mexicans," he explained. "I booked a trip there to see if I could find it."

"How did you plan to locate the money, Aymard?"

Caron's face tightened. Every time the old man said his name, it felt like a barbed whip striking his back. And he didn't quite understand why it felt that way. Something about his tone of voice.

Caron swallowed and said, "No idea. I thought I'd wait for somebody else to find it and, you know, take it from them."

Page grunted again.

"Now, do you mind telling me what you're thinking?" Caron asked, adding after, "Sir?"

Jean-Bernard Page blinked a few times, his eyes not leaving the man in the bed.

Caron watched him back.

"We suspect," the big boss began, "that somebody sold you out in an attempt to remove you from the hierarchy."

"If they'd waited, the Americans might have done it for them."

"Uh-huh. Perhaps they wanted *exactly* that. How many people knew of that chalet of yours, Aymard?"

"Including people in this room?"

Page shrugged.

"The three of us. Unless Adalene made a phone call—"

"That's a lie," Adalene said, barely raising her voice.

"She didn't call," Page said. "Whoever tipped off the Americans sent an email."

Caron looked up at the ceiling. He blinked a few times. An idea started forming in his head.

"Wait a minute," he said, looking back at the big boss. "Email? That means computers."

Adalene quipped, "At least we know your brain is still functioning."

"Stop it," he snapped back. "Computers. Who in the organization uses computers more than the rest of us?"

Page's head raised a little, and Caron suspected the same idea was forming in his mind, too.

"Crisfulli," Page said.

"The bastard," Caron said. "It's *him* and his woman we should be after. *She* might have sent the email."

The short, old man turned to the woman. "What do you think?"

"I think Caron wasn't expected to survive," Adalene said, "so somebody's plan has been derailed ever so slightly."

"Do you think he's right?"

"I think if Caron is right," Adalene continued, "our Ceasario will make a move against Cote soon enough. He needs to get rid of her before he can get to you."

Page nodded. "I should have figured it was Ceasario. I knew someday this would happen. He's been waiting a long time."

"Care to explain?" Adalene asked.

"No," Page said.

"Crisfulli will go after the money," Caron said.

"How do you know?"

"Maybe we talked about it?"

"Maybe," the old man said. "Maybe you conspired together, perhaps?"

"If I was helping him, why would he kill me?"

"There are things you don't know, Aymard. Ceasario has his reasons."

"But you're not telling."

"No."

Silence lingered a moment. Caron said, "If he's going after Desire, or arranging for the Americans to do it for him, we should have somebody waiting when that happens."

"That's a *very* good idea," said Adalene Severin.

A hot flush crawled up Caron's neck when he noticed she didn't add "sir". And then he had another idea. "What if Cote is with Crisfulli in this scheme?"

"Well," Page said, "I suppose we have to consider that, don't we? What would you suggest we do, Aymard?"

"A little spring cleaning, sir," Caron said.

Page nodded. "It is necessary from time to time, yes. We can't have dirty windows and all that." To Adalene: "See to it."

Adalene Severin nodded once.

"Starting with him." Page left the room.

Caron thrashed against his restraints. "Wait! No! I didn't betray you!"

Adalene Severin took out a pistol from her purse and shot Aymard Caron once in the head. His protests stopped forever.

Nassau

"I didn't appreciate you hanging up on me, Reaper."

"It's been a rough day, ma'am."

"Sounds like it's getting rougher."

"Get me an ID on those pictures I sent you," Kane said. He sat on the edge of the bed in his hotel room, the cell phone to his right ear. He looked at the carpet and wondered how soft it was but didn't want to remove his shoes to find out. He wasn't staying any longer than it took to update Thurston.

"Was that a please I heard?"

"We can discuss my attitude later, ma'am."

"Wait one," Thurston said. "Or more."

Kane didn't reply. Thurston placed him on hold. Thankfully there was no hold music, only silence. Kane stared at the carpet. He hadn't wanted to spoil his time with Don and Katie, so he'd kept his reaction to Luna Blaise's death in check, but the news weighed on him. *Another one down. How many more?*

Thurston came back on the line.

"You still there?"

"Haven't moved, ma'am."

"You know Lorenzo, and we confirmed the Corridor tie-up, so there's our connection. Still, plenty of questions to answer, though."

"Like who sent the email, right. What about Barrel Chest?"

"Even Slick was surprised how quickly his identity turned up once we ran the photo," Thurston said. "His name is Brad Chandler. Ring any bells?"

Kane had to think. Nothing came to mind right away. Then: "Mercenary, right?"

"Correct. Hired gun to the cartels, mostly."

"Do I get the rest of the team?"

"No," Thurston said. "They're busy. I want you to observe only. Take no direct action."

"No promises, ma'am."

"I'm not kidding, Reaper."

"They're already making moves against us," Kane said, explaining about the Mercedes that followed Mateo's car from the airport. "They know we're here. It's only a matter of time before the pizza hits the fan."

"I don't want any pizza near any fans, Reaper."

"Are we done, ma'am?"

"Perhaps in more ways than one," Thurston said, ending the call.

Kane cursed and put his phone away. He left the room. Time to get back downstairs and do his best to follow orders.

Because all he wanted to do right now was tear some limbs from any cartel beast he could find.

Vengeance may not bring about any peace, but releasing the rage boiling inside him might do some good after all.

CHAPTER 9

Carlos Lorenzo certainly had the better of the two deals.

Fresh popcorn crunched in his mouth as he sat under the awning of the Nassau racetrack, watching a group of jockeys fling their horses around a short loop. He didn't have any money on this race; probably wasn't going to bet all day. He loved horses. He loved fast horses in particular. All he wanted to really do was watch the animals. If one came up that seemed worth betting on, he'd drop a few bucks, but money, in this case, wasn't his goal.

The air was crisp, the sky clear; no ocean in sight, but the track was nestled in an area of rich green, so that was nice too.

He would much rather be in Nassau than across the world in London where his friend Ceasario was taking care of his side of the plan. Lorenzo's job was to get all the ducks lined up, i.e., people, boats, plot out the search area, secure a safehouse, all the technical matters. Some of his tasks, most having been accomplished, had to wait until Ceasario and Bella Lane arrived with Leland Bascomb. And Lorenzo hoped that Bascomb provided the free pass they'd need from the Nassau governing bodies in order to search their territory for buried treasure.

The idea made Carlos Lorenzo laugh. Buried treasure. The stuff of legends was finally reality. Ceasario said the map he'd recovered from Mexico was undeniably the real deal, not a false clue planted as a rabbit trail.

Lorenzo certainly hoped his friend was right. He wanted to see Ceasario achieve the vengeance long denied him; he also wanted to personally benefit from the leadership changes in the French-Italian Corridor that Ceasario would carry out. He looked forward to taking his promotion with relish.

He'd spent so much time as one of the lower-echelon operators in Ceasario's team, bringing in countless amounts of money and keeping smuggling points secured, he certainly felt he deserved a higher spot on the refreshed totem pole.

Lorenzo's attention was so fixed on the racing thoroughbreds that he didn't realize he was being watched.

By three people only a few rows away.

"You said he normally shows up alone?" Kane asked.

"Yeah, he never talks with anybody when the horses are running," Don Mateo said. He sat next to Kane, with Reaper on his right; Katie sat to his left.

"I think we've seen him here," Katie said, wearing sunglasses despite a wide-brimmed hat, "four times already. Always alone."

"I get it," Kane said.

They sat six rows behind Lorenzo with an unobstructed view of the back of his head. Most of the race watchers were standing in the inside promenade, the level of which almost matched the track, and included video screens and easy access to various bars and restaurants within the building. Kane had a race card in his hand, to which he casually referred out of genuine interest in the horses. He'd prefer to watch cars race, but anything fast caught his attention, and the horses certainly provided a reason engine power was measured in *horse*power. Those animals might give a tricked-out Corvette a run for the money.

The horse that had Kane's wish for a win was named Chin-N-Tonic, out of Ireland, and the white mare was holding her own in second place but quickly edging on first-place holder Magic Charles.

As the group of horses rounded the track, heading for the finish, Chin-N-Tonic's jockey put his head down, and the horse surged ahead with a burst of power that put her at least a neck ahead of Magic Charles.

Magic Charles seemed out of gas at that point. He held steady, but not enough to keep Chin-N-Tonic from easing out further in front, and by the time the horses crossed the finish line, the winner was Chin-N-Tonic.

"I should have dropped fifty on that one," Kane said. He turned the page to examine the names for the next race. "You say this guy Lorenzo has been meeting other cartel people."

"Yeah."

"Where are they at?"

"Probably the beach house."

"Excuse me?"

"We followed them a few times," Katie said.

"Hell, Don, that's how they caught onto you."

"Whoops," Mateo said. He was smiling.

"Where's this beach house?" Kane asked.

"On the coast, we'll go and look at it," Mateo said.

"I wonder if the rest of Chandler's mercenary crew is at the house, too," Kane said.

"Probably. Ever come across that guy?"

"Have you?"

"Once, in the Middle East actually," Mateo said.

"Any remarks?"

"I should have killed him when I had the chance."

"Why?"

"He wasn't there because of a job, he was there stealing Iraqi antiques to sell on the black market," Mateo said. "One night, my crew and I were out at dinner, and he was in the same spot with his crew, and everybody was getting drunk and rowdy, and he tried to rape a random woman there too, right in front of everybody. Me and a couple of my guys pulled him off her and dealt with the situation. His buddies had to carry him out. That's all I need to know about him. He's not a nice person."

Katie said, "And that's putting it mildly."

"Were you there too?" Kane asked.

"Don and I had just started dating," she said.

"You two have the most interesting dates," Kane said.

"What about you?" Mateo asked. "Anybody sharing your foxhole?"

"No."

Mateo started to say more, but a nudge from his wife closed his mouth.

The next round of horses lined up at the gates. A starter pistol cracked, the gates opened, and the horses plunged full speed onto the track.

Kane glanced once more at his program and decided he liked a horse named Horsey McHorseFace, from Australia. He excused himself to place a bet, not a huge amount, but enough that if he won, he could buy lunch for Don and Katie.

The horse came in fifth.

The seaside villa housing the rest of Lorenzo's motley crew wasn't far from the resort, off West Bay Street. Only a seawall protected the property from the crashing ocean waves. Beyond the wall was a wide yard, well taken care of, with green grass and healthy palm trees, the house itself a single-story with lots of glass and a wrap-around porch. It was far enough away from neighboring villas to be what one might call "secluded", certainly far enough away from prying eyes that nobody seemed to notice the man on the porch with a pistol on his hip.

Nearby construction on open lots distracted from the ocean view. Once, when Nassau was solely the playground of the rich, and area could survive on the niche trade those celebrities provided. Now, the economy depended on much more business, tourists from all walks of life from around the world, which meant more hotels, more rental properties, more everything. And, as a result, less open space, fewer views of the water without sitting literally on the beach. The economy of Nassau in particular and the Bahamas, in general, might prosper, but in the process, it lost something too, that original splendor so admired by the first visitors who made it a point to keep coming back. If they showed up now, they probably wouldn't recognize the place.

"I love how the guard advertises his weapon," Kane said. "Makes my job so much easier."

"Right?" Mateo said.

Kane sat in the back seat of Mateo's BMW, behind Mateo in the driver's seat, the tinted window rolled down.

Kane snapped pictures, zooming as close as his digital camera permitted. They were parked curbside almost a block away from the villa, next to an empty lot that had not yet been cleared for construction.

Kane snapped another picture. None of the pictures were good enough to get a facial scan from, but Kane figured they didn't need any more evidence. Lorenzo cinched the deal. The French-Italian Corridor had something to do with the treasure hunt in Nassau, and now they needed to figure out how everything tied together, and especially who was in charge. Kane didn't think for a minute that Carlos Lorenzo was calling the shots. He was a worker bee.

The villa, though, offered a lot of protection, the wrap-around porch providing an excellent observation point for the water and the front, but the abundance of windows to maximize every view possible was certainly a weak spot, and not necessarily for any assault Kane might lead. He could see them; they could see him. A sneak attack was more or less out of the question unless they employed some distractive pyrotechnics first. Lorenzo had chosen well. Kane still wanted to know the strength of his force, but he'd figure that out, probably first hand soon enough.

"I'm curious," Katie said. "How *would* you attack a place like that?"

"Very carefully," Kane said.

"Seriously."

"My orders are to observe and report," Kane said. "If I start thinking about direct action, I might start getting naughty ideas."

"Remember—" Mateo said.

"Don't start," Kane snapped.

Katie laughed. It took a moment, but Kane did too. It felt good to laugh after his earlier black mood.

Mateo said, "Car coming."

Kane watched through the viewfinder. The car was a small four-door sedan with four women inside. He focused on the logo on the driver's door, which showed a bucket crisscrossed with two mops and the name Quick Cleaning Service. "Housekeepers," Kane said. "Know the place?" He read out the name on the side of the car.

"They're downtown, yeah," Mateo said.

Kane watched the four women get out of the car. The driver unlocked the trunk and began handing out cleaning supplies and giving directions. She was short, pudgy in the middle, no makeup, long hair. She gave directions to the other three women as they approach the front door. The guard stood off to the side while they entered the villa. He watched them curiously, not lecherously. They were expected, and he had no reason to block their entry.

Which meant they'd visited the house several times already, which meant they knew every corner of the place, which meant, well, a whole lot of things and John Kane suddenly wanted to have a chat with the pudgy boss lady.

"I think I'm getting an idea," Kane said. "Let's get out of here."

Mateo started the car.

Brad Chandler dried off his stocky body from a shower and started dressing, catching sight, as he often did, of the Marine Corps "Semper Fidelis" tattoo on his right shoulder.

He was an American who had served his country for over 15 years before taking off on his own. He'd joined the military because running with gangs at home was a sure-fire ticket to prison, and he thought he could score much better while wearing a uniform — the military had all kinds of neat stuff to steal, a ready black market for enterprising young men who knew how to take advantage. He'd been lucky not to end up in the stockade. Chandler used the Corps as a way to enrich himself, using the black market to sell everything from small arms to intelligence products ferreted out by his own spies at the Pentagon. He'd built his network as the foundation of his mercenary career and now hired out to the highest bidder for whatever the task, from overthrowing a country to assassination. His network kept him appraised of potential pitfalls, and so far, he had remained one step ahead of Western intelligence authorities who would certainly like his head mounted on a wall.

In the last few years, he'd found most of his work with the drug cartels of Central America and Mexico, but recent efforts by American law enforcement had sent a lot of his employers to prison or the grave, so he'd had to advertise his services elsewhere.

Luckily, the European drug networks were as hungry for a good shooter as their south of the border counterparts.

The current mission with Ceasario Crisfulli had seemed like a fantasy at first, a typical buried treasure fool's scenario. But the more Chandler learned, the more he saw up close with Crisfulli's operatives in the region, the more he realized this was no wild goose chase or con job. The Sanchez money was real, they were going to find it, and he was going to get a piece of it, along with protection promised by Crisfulli should he ever be in need of a place to hide.

Not that he believed that part of the deal, but Chandler was willing to give Crisfulli the benefit of the doubt. Crisfulli knew Chandler's reputation well enough to also know he'd be killed unmercifully if he pulled a double-cross. But Chandler knew the purpose of the money, and what Crisfulli had in mind for his former colleagues, and it wasn't simply a case of turning on associates for personal gain. Crisfulli had a reason; he had an agenda; vengeance was at the top of his mind, and Chandler didn't blame him for being pissed off.

He heard the front door of the villa open, and the cleaning ladies announce themselves. He hurried to finish drying off, then quickly dressed. His black T-shirt fit around his barrel chest snugly, and he looked ripped. Down the hall in his bedroom, he pulled on some boots, then wandered out to the main room.

He had three men with him on this job. Jackson, on guard duty outside; and Rosen, who sat in the couch in the living room reading on his tablet computer. The cleaning crew and their pudgy boss, who looked quite cute despite her usual lack of makeup, began separating to cover various areas of the house. Chandler said hello, but none of the women looked at him. He'd told his men they were hands off, and he had a feeling the women didn't feel quite secure around such brutes. He didn't blame them one bit. In the kitchen, he grabbed a coffee and went to sit out on the back patio while the ladies did their work.

He chose a chair near the wooden railing, with a nice view of the ocean, even though the seawall blocked part of the view. Water was water; he'd seen it a million times. He showered under water at least once a day; often, he even drank water. Water was nothing new to him. He'd already had his daily swim, and a practice session with their SCUBA gear; now it was time to relax. The crashing waves helped him relax. The rhythm of the waves settled his mind.

It wasn't long before Rosen joined him, still carrying his tablet computer. Rosen was taller and thinner than Chandler, wiry instead of ripped, but just as deadly as his boss with a rifle, pistol, or his hands. Rosen liked to avoid high explosives. He let Jackson handle anything that needed blowing up real good.

Rosen was an Israeli army reject who'd seen more than his share of action and had the same larcenous spirit as Chandler.

"How long till Crisfulli gets here?" Rosen asked.

Chandler checked his watch. "Should be any minute. You getting anxious?"

Rosen scoffed. "You mean do I actually want to work soon?"

"The soft life can get to you," Chandler said. "If it weren't for the swimming we've been doing, I think we'd have gone nuts by now. Been a long two weeks."

During those two weeks, they'd mostly done busy work with Carlos Lorenzo, securing a yacht, diving equipment, and other items related to the underwater search. Since Chandler and his men were the ones going under the water to find the money, they'd spent a lot of time with practice dives and calibrating their SCUBA gear.

The yacht they'd acquired was a nice one, an Evo 43 with a large rear deck, and platforms that rose or extended depending on the need. They'd have plenty of working room and storage space for gear when they finally hit the ocean.

They'd also been renting small motorboats from the local marina to test an underwater drone, a PowerRay Explorer Underwater Robot, that Chandler controlled by remote. The camera at the front of the drone sent back images onto a laptop that were as crystal clear as could be desired. They'd be using the drone to check for where the treasure was supposed to be before making any attempt at diving to recover the loot. They expected the dive to require more immersion than a recreational SCUBA dive, and they only wanted to drop beneath the ocean surface once.

Playing with new toys was always fun, but Chandler was itching for real work.

A real fight.

"What are you going to do with your share of the money?" Rosen asked.

Chandler shrugged. "Buy a new car?"

Jackson laughed. "I'll build an underground lair and make plans to conquer the world."

"Then what?"

"I'll forget about them because with all that money, who cares?"

Chandler glanced over his shoulder to see the pudgy boss lady wiping down the glass coffee table in the sitting area. She had to keep brushing back her hair when it dropped in front of her face. Finally, she stood up long enough to tie it back, lifting her shirt long enough in the process to expose her belly button.

Chandler grinned.

Rosen looked too.

Rosen asked, "You getting ideas?"

"No," Chandler said, "I don't like them here."

"Part of the rental agreement."

"But what are they saying to each other when they leave? Our gear isn't here, sure, but we aren't living like regular tourists."

"Let our boss deal with that." Rosen looked back again. "In the meantime, dibs on the short one."

Chandler faced forward again. The women were security risks, for sure, but their daily presence also made Chandler and his crew hide anything that looked remotely unlawful. "Sure," he said.

Jackson shouted from around the corner.

"Look alive, boss is pulling up."

Chandler and Rosen went back inside.

CHAPTER 10

It's amazing what one can do when the Sword of Damocles hangs over his family.

Leland Bascomb resigned himself to cooperating with Crisfulli and not resisting in any way. Hearing about the details of the treasure hunt almost took his mind off the horror of his wife being held hostage and the threat hanging over his sons, but the distraction did not last long.

Crisfulli needed him for a specific task, and then he would no longer be of use.

That meant only one thing.

He didn't trust for a minute that Crisfulli would simply let him go. No way. Bascomb had to cooperate in the meantime, but his mind was racing, thinking of escape, looking for the right moment.

But that moment wasn't going to happen at the airport, as they stepped off the private jet. Crisfulli had the woman, Bella Lane, and two strongarm types who eyed him like they expected trouble. At some point, Crisfulli would need to ditch the guard dogs. They couldn't very well have their "type" hanging around government offices where somebody's crap detector would start going off. Then, maybe, an escape opportunity could present itself. He knew the governor's building well. They'd have to travel there to get the proper exploring permits and pay required fees. Bascomb decided that visit was his best chance.

They'd at least removed the shackles and provided a suitcase containing clothing that Crisfulli claimed properly fit. Bascomb knew better than to ask how Crisfulli had learned his size. And if he knew that much, what else did he know? Suddenly Bascomb didn't feel as confident about finding a way out during the visit to the government house. And what would happen to his family once he escaped?

Bascomb sighed once they entered the terminal building and began the formalities with the customs people.

Escape might not be possible, after all.

But he refused to give up hope. There had been times, on the ocean, in the middle of nowhere, when it seemed like he wouldn't make it home. Mechanical breakdowns had often left him, and his crew, stranded, requiring not just skill to overcome, but improvisation. Violent storms, a constant on the open seas, had many times threatened to end his life and the lives of his crew.

Bascomb had always prevailed because of a repeated mantra. *Don't panic. Stay focused. Work the problem.*

He needed the same resolve in this situation.

The two guards took the front seat, one driving, while Crisfulli, Bella Lane, and Bascomb sat in the back seat. They were in a bigger car than the one used in London, so they weren't as pressed together in the back.

It made the ride a little more comfortable.

Ceasario Crisfulli thought he had Bascomb sufficiently

subdued, but the man's alert eyes were used to looking for every last detail. The man might prove to be trouble after all, and Crisfulli hoped the threat over the man's wife and sons kept him in line. He hadn't been lying when he'd promised not to hurt the man as long as he cooperated, but if Bascomb did anything stupid, Crisfulli would have to respond.

Crisfulli wasn't an animal. Mindless killing proved nothing, accomplished nothing, and only brought trouble. The only people he wanted to kill were ones who deserved killing. His list had only one name, one man who needed killing, but those standing between Crisfulli and that man had to die too. Any blood lust running through his veins, he knew, was best reserved for the final battle when he'd need it most.

The scenic route meant nothing to him as the driver took them away from the airport and to the coastal safe-house. His mind wasn't on the sights, even though he heard Bella Lane's enthusiastic outbursts whenever she saw something of note. His mind was on the mission. The money. His crew in Nassau, led by Carlos Lorenzo, should have completed their tasks, that of securing a boat, necessarily diving equipment, and an underwater drone to check out the suspected treasure site before they sent down the divers.

With any luck, they'd be in and out of Nassau within 48 hours.

News of Caron's "rescue" in Paris had reached him during the flight from London. The White Wolf was doing exactly as Crisfulli had predicted. He had hoped the Americans might remove Caron, but he had misjudged their ultimate intentions. They should have killed him while rescuing their compatriot. They hadn't. Perhaps the White Wolf had obliged instead. If the old man sensed treachery, he wouldn't hesitate to kill anybody he suspected, even if they were entirely innocent.

He *had* formed an alliance with Aymard Caron early on, tempting Caron into a 50/50 split of what Crisfulli said would be "found money", and for their use only. Crisfulli had needed Caron's financial help in paying for Chandler and his two men, and for the purchase of other incidentals that he didn't want traced back to him. Caron fulfilled his obligations around the time the Americans began their campaign and provided Crisfulli with the perfect way to eliminate his "friend" before he had to do it himself.

Caron might put the pieces together and figure out it was his "buddy" who tried to get rid of him, and he'd run his mouth until the White Wolf granted him the blessing of killing Crisfulli in retaliation. But Ceasario knew the White Wolf better than anyone. He'd understand Crisfulli's unspoken motivation, the reason for the treachery to begin with, which truly had nothing to do with the money, and that meant Caron was fish food. No doubt. The only question Crisfulli had was wondering how the old man put everything together once the truth dawned on him, knowing his day of reckoning had finally arrived, and that he should have killed Crisfulli long ago, instead of humiliating him with a leadership position meant to keep him contained?

Because the man thought he was God, and not even Crisfulli would try and kill God.

How the situation must have amused him over the years, Crisfulli thought. But the old man had no idea that Ceasario knew how to bide his time, look for an opportunity, even if it took decades.

But with Caron out of the picture, Crisfulli had to assume that the White Wolf's despicable black widow, Adalene Severin, would be leaving the sanctuary to try and find him. It meant the old man might have decided to liquidate Desire Cote. It meant that between the Americans and the old man's paranoia, Crisfulli would be able to march right to the old man's front door without opposition. *And the Wolf thought he was brilliant. God never made mistakes.*

As the driver made the final turn to the safehouse, Crisfulli cleared his mind of questions. He had a job to do. Everything else could wait.

He'd been waiting a long time already. A little longer wasn't going to hurt.

Brad Chandler told the cleaning crew to hurry.

The women kept their heads down and mouths shut as they hurried to finish the cleaning, and when Crisfulli and his party parked in the driveway, Chandler stood out front to greet them.

"Welcome to Nassau," Chandler said.

Crisfulli looked over Chandler's shoulder.

"Who are they?"

"Cleaning crew," Chandler said. "Part of the rental."

Crisfulli raised an eyebrow.

"I told them to hurry up," the mercenary said. "They'll be gone shortly."

"I want them gone now."

"Yes, sir."

Chandler turned and re-entered the house, Crisfulli and his people behind him. He told the cleaning ladies to pack up their crap and get out. He raised his voice to do so, and the wide eyes received in return told him they weren't going to argue. The boss lady started snapping rapid Spanish, the girls collected their supplies, and left the house much more quickly than even Chandler expected. When their little car had driven away, Crisfulli finally relaxed.

"Put up the map."

"Yes, sir."

Chandler and Rosen pinned a large map of the area on a bare wall near the kitchen. Crisfulli ignored the mercs as he and another older man began to examine the map. The woman remained aloof, the guards near her, but she held a metal box. Chandler bet that box contained the location of the money they were after. Chandler also figured the other guy was the expert ocean explorer Lorenzo had said was coming. He hung back with Jackson and Rosen as the boss did the talking.

Crisfulli told the woman to hand him the box. She did. He opened the box and took out a piece of paper. He handed the paper to the Brit. "Find this spot on the map."

The Brit said okay and consulted both the notes on the paper and the map. He looked at a wide area off the coast, at least thirty miles away. "Right here," the Brit said. "They aren't on this map, but there is a cluster of rocks that stick above the surface. There are caves and other nooks under the water. Your treasure is somewhere there."

"How many caves?"

"I never explored the area."

"But you should have heard from others."

"It was never something I was interested in, Mr. Crisfulli. I don't know how many caves."

"Fair enough." Crisfulli asked Chandler for a pen. Chandler retrieved one from a drawer in the kitchen. Crisfulli used the pen to write an X on the map. Chandler stifled a laugh. *X marks the spot, why not?*

Crisfulli said to the Brit, "I want you to take a shower, get cleaned up, and put on the suit we packed for you.

We're going to the government house in forty-five minutes. We need permits and permissions to explore this area. I cannot have any interference from coastal authorities."

The Brit nodded sharply. Chandler ordered Rosen to show the Brit to the bathroom.

Carlos Lorenzo sat near the pool at the resort, waiting for Crisfulli to arrive. The pool was nowhere near as relaxing as the horse track. He'd rather have met the boss there, but orders were orders, or something like that, and Lorenzo wasn't one to argue anyway. As he sat alone at a table and watched the activity around the pool, he could only think one thing:

Jeeezzusssss wept, why did fat men need to wear tiny speedos? Why did women who had no business wearing a bikini — and he wasn't talking about older broads, either, but 20 to 30 somethings who were still young — do so and show off their expanding middles and the fact that all they did was eat rubbish and drink alcohol and thus make the Pillsbury Doughboy nervous because he might lose his job to one of these roly-poly chicks who would work cheaper and still have all the required jelly rolls?

Not that he could talk, really. His middle was expanding a little too. The soft life was a killer. But Lorenzo figured he had earned soft time, after years of hustling his way to the top of the French-Italian Corridor, and not even the top, really. More like a few levels down from the top. Close enough to the top, anyway, that he could relax a little, and have younger men than he handle all the hustling. All he needed to do was keep them in line and pass the cash they collected up the food chain to the White Wolf.

Back home, there were true beauties to occupy his

attention when he wasn't watching racing. Here in the Bahamas? Not so much. Some of the females caught his eye, but not enough. He'd rather watch the horses.

"Enjoying yourself?"

Lorenzo didn't have to turn and look. He stood up and greeted the man in the white suit with a hug and gestured to an empty chair. Crisfulli sat and scooted close.

"What are you drinking?" Crisfulli asked.

"Rum-and-Coke."

Crisfulli signaled to a passing waiter and ordered the same.

"Where do we stand?" Crisfulli asked.

"Everything is arranged," Lorenzo said. The waiter brought Crisfulli's drink midway through the description of the boat Lorenzo had acquired, and as Crisfulli took his first sip, Lorenzo concluded with details on Chandler and his two mercenaries practicing with the diving equipment.

"Excellent," Crisfulli said. "We had a good afternoon at the government house. Permits are squared away. Bascomb is so far worth the trouble."

"He didn't try to escape or make a fuss?"

"No, were you expecting something?"

"You can never tell with a hostage."

Crisfulli agreed, knowing Lorenzo knew more about using hostages to achieve goals than he did. He said, "Bascomb behaved himself. His eyes were a little shifty for a while, and maybe he had something in mind, a way to get somebody's attention, but it was so busy I think he gave up."

"More than likely," Lorenzo said, "he gave up because the staff has turned over several times since his last visit, and he had nobody to yell for."

"We also have his family."

"There's that, too."

"How are things here? Any trouble?"

"Some," Lorenzo said.

Crisfulli raised an eyebrow and took another drink.

"Two Americans, and now a third," Lorenzo said. "They aren't official agents, at least the first two."

"Who are the first two?"

"From what we can gather, a couple on vacation, both of which have military backgrounds."

"And the third?"

"The male half of the couple collected the third man from the airport yesterday. I had Chandler and Rosen follow them for a while."

"Where are they staying?"

"This resort. The woman is sitting over there, watching us probably."

Crisfulli let out a chuckle. "Tell me more, Carlos," he said

Katie Mateo didn't get nervous until Lorenzo, and the new man, started speaking in hushed tones.

That's when she stowed her camera back in her purse and left the patio area. She used the tourists for cover and slipped back into the lobby. Finding her husband and Kane in one of the lobby bars, she joined them at the table and called up the pictures on her phone.

"New guy?" Kane asked. He and Don sat with beers in front of them.

"I only got one shot at his face," she said. "I think our friend Carlos told him where I was sitting."

"How do you know?"

"Spidey sense?" she said.

"Good enough for me," Kane replied.

She showed Kane the pic of Crisfulli. Don leaned over for a peek too.

"Know him?" Don Mateo asked.

"Something about that white suit rings a bell," Kane said. "Send it to my phone."

Katie tapped the screen a few times and complied.

Kane took out his own phone and forwarded the picture to headquarters.

Team Reaper Jet
En Route to Europe

Cara Billings ignored the chatter from her colleagues as the jet carried them over the ocean. She sat in a leather chair next to a window, looking out at the horizon over the tip of the right wing. The rest of the team, including Kane's replacement, sat around a table playing poker.

She wished Kane were with them. As much as her tough exterior might suggest otherwise, and their personal situation notwithstanding, she saw him as the team's rock. The man to count on. The one who might not have all the answers but had enough. She knew the rest of the team felt the same way. In the meantime, General Thurston had appointed Pete Traynor to fill Kane's shoes, and that was fine with Cara. The ex-DEA agent was a very capable operator and an asset to Team Reaper. He was almost as tall as Cara, his unshaven face a constant feature, along with the tattoos on his arms.

They were on their way to Montenegro and the casino run by Corridor associate Desire Cote, the second name on their Corridor target list. Cote controlled the syndicate's money laundering efforts via the casino. They were going after her first, rather than Ceasario Crisfulli, because their inquiries had turned up no sign of Crisfulli. He wasn't anywhere near his usual haunts and hadn't been spotted elsewhere in the world. Thurston decided they'd go after Cote first. She was in charge of the money, so, if she and Crisfulli were working together, or if he was manipulating the Corridor leadership for his own purposes, perhaps they'd find that connection through the woman. The money to fund a takeover effort had to come from somewhere while they searched for the Sanchez treasure, which Cara still thought was a pipe dream, the kind of rumor shared by cartel thugs when pulling guard duty late at night after they had no more women to talk about.

And if Cote was a dead end, Cara might finally start complaining out loud.

"Aces and eights!" Brick called out.

Axe, Arenas, and Traynor groaned and threw their useless cards into the center of the table while Brick collected a pile of chips.

Cara watched them for a second, then turned her attention back to the view from the window.

Aces and eights.

The dead man's hand.

She tried to ignore the chill that crawled up her neck.

Nassau

"Does the name Ceasario Crisfulli mean anything to you?"

Kane frowned as he considered General Thurston's question.

"I knew I remembered the white suit," he said. "Second or third in the Corridor flow chart."

"Third," Thurston said. "Crisfulli's been hard to pin down, nobody knows where he is, so Cara and the others are going after Desire Cote to see if there's a connection on her end. Of course, as soon as they're halfway across the ocean, Slick finally finds something. Crisfulli and his girlfriend, Bella Lane, were last seen in London. Facial scan picked them up. They weren't traveling under their real names."

"Something happen in London?"

"An ocean expert name Leland Bascomb has gone missing," she said.

"He's one of those Cousteau-types, right? Television shows and books with lots of pictures and all that?"

"Exactly. The university he teaches made the report. His family hasn't been much help."

"Sounds like we'll find Bascomb in Nassau, and his family needs rescuing."

"I'll send it up the flagpole," Thurston said. "Meanwhile, I think we've found our answer to the sender of the email and everything else. The woman, Bella Lane, is a computer expert. She'd be able to send that email along the route it took to get to you and make sure we couldn't trace it after the fact."

"I might need some toys, ma'am."

"Care package on the way. We're beyond surveillance now. Don't get arrested."

"I'll do my best. And have Slick dig into Crisfulli's background. See if there's a reason why he'd want to knock over the White Wolf at this point in his life."

"Already on it. We do function without you, Reaper."

"And you can continue to do so, is that it?"

"We'll talk when you get back."

"You're assuming I'm coming back." Kane killed the connection as anger flashed through him. She was really pissing him off. She might have a reason, sure, Kane's attitude had been lousy lately, downright insubordinate, but it might have helped matters if she'd asked how he was doing instead of being all "general" about matters. Maybe then he'd explain his recent frustrations. Maybe then she'd understand, and they could have a different conversation. Or, maybe, he could quit being a hard case and tell her himself. Communication was a two-way street, after all. And Thurston wasn't a mind reader.

Kane suddenly felt like a jerk. He'd explain and correct the behavior the next time they talked.

But, yeah, they had their answer. Crisfulli was the bad guy they were looking for, the one going after Sanchez's buried millions, the one scheming to knock off his competition on the way to the top of the French-Italian Corridor.

As Kane returned to the lobby via the elevator, he wondered if Crisfulli wasn't laughing at the thought of Reaper doing most of his dirty work.

It was time to show him just how dirty Team Reaper could play.

"We have a hostage situation," Kane explained to Don and Katie Mateo. They had left the hotel to take a walk on the beach, pausing now and then. All three were continuously scanning the area for threats. They paused near a palm tree that provided a break from the sun's glare. It also put them in the middle of a crowd so anybody not wearing a bathing suit or shorts would stand out. It was hard to hide a submachine gun in a pair of swim trunks. *Hey, babe, is that a Micro-Uzi in your trunks or are you really happy to see me?*

"Who's the hostage?" Don asked.

Kane explained about the disappearance in London of Leland Bascomb.

"Why would they take him?" Katie asked.

"He's known in these parts," Kane said. "He's a celebrity ocean explorer. It's the perfect cover Crisfulli needs to go look for the Sanchez money. He can hang back and be merely an 'investor' while Bascomb does the work."

"They might have him at the house," Don said.

"You're positive that's their only gathering point?"

"It's the only one they've ever gone to," Don said.

"All right," Kane said. "Our best source of intel will be the cleaning ladies."

"Do you know where to find them?" Katie asked.

"No, but we can stake out the cleaning office and wait for them to go home for the day."

"What if it's a different crew today?" Katie asked.

"Then we watch for the boss lady from yesterday. She's the one I remember. Who's driving?"

Don volunteered.

During the drive to the Quick Cleaning Service office in a nearby shopping center, Kane and Don pointed out that none of the drug thugs had been following them since Kane's arrival. They might not have needed to follow them any longer. They might have been too busy. Crisfulli might have been planning for how to get rid of the three of them before going after the treasure.

Which meant they needed to keep their eyes open.

Kane was carrying the SIG M17 pistol under his windbreaker and trying not to look like an idiot wearing a jacket in an area where shorts and loose shirts were the normal attire for males not at the beach. But if the enemy brought the fight to them, they had to have a way to respond, at least until Kane's "care package" arrived.

They staked out the Quick Cleaning Service for the remainder of the afternoon; when the car containing the boss lady they'd seen previously at the enemy villa, Kane pointed out the woman in charge. Short, thick in the middle, her hair no longer tied back, and cascading down her shoulders.

The woman spent a few minutes inside, then exited alone to climb into an old Ford truck.

Don Mateo followed the truck.

The woman drove to a grocery store and parked. Kane and Katie followed her inside. Don remained with the car.

"Need anything?" Kane asked as they entered the air-conditioned store. It looked like any number of grocery stores all over the world; full of aisles containing items for sale, locals pushing carts, mothers dealing with rowdy kids.

"I could use grapes," Katie said. She and Kane headed for the produce section, where the woman was examining a display of apples.

"Cold approach?" Katie asked.

"What the heck," Kane said.

Katie Mateo stood back while Kane closed the distance.

"Hi," he said.

The woman looked at him oddly. Kane figured she had no idea what to make of the intrusion.

"My name's John Kane. I'm with the US government."

"So?"

"There's a villa you're cleaning," he said, explaining the location, so she knew what he was talking about, and then asking: "We think the men renting the house are drug smugglers. Can you tell us what's going on inside?"

The woman stepped back, a hand to her chest.

"Oh my God," she said. "Are you serious?"

"Yeah."

"Do you have a badge or something?"

"No, ma'am."

"You're *that* kind of government?"

"Sure." He had no idea what she meant. If she wanted to believe he was a man in black, why not?

She leaned close. "There is something *bad* in that house."

"Tell me."

"Who is she?"

Kane glanced back at Katie, who had stepped closer.

"That's my associate. Her name is Katie."

"My name is Francesca," the woman said. "I've been cleaning houses for years and years, and I'm telling you, there is something bad in that villa."

"What happened today?"

"We were doing our usual routine. The landlord pays us to be there every day; he especially wants to make sure renters don't destroy the place. The tourists aren't what they used to be. Lots of slobs and young people now who have too much money and no respect for other people's property."

"Right."

"I was going down the hall to clean the bedrooms, and one door was locked. The big man, the one who seems to be in charge, told me not to clean in there. I told him the landlord says we have to, and he looked like he was going to hit me and told me not to go in there."

"What did you do?"

"I didn't go in there. But I *heard* something inside."

Kane waited.

"It sounded like somebody moaning."

"Which room did you say that was?"

Francesca described the hallway layout and which side the locked room was on. "All the way down, the last room on the right."

Kane nodded. Probably where they were keeping Leland Bascomb.

"Does a man in a white suit hang around? He'll have a girlfriend with him."

"The redhead? I've only seen them once yesterday. I don't know where they are staying. But the three men who have been there a while, they are still there. They are always suspicious and covering things they don't want us to see."

"Have you noticed, in the bedrooms, if there are any wires near the windows?"

She frowned in thought, then shook her head. "No, I haven't noticed anything like that."

No boobytraps. Good.

Kane took out his wallet. "Francesca, do you mind if the United States pays for your groceries today?"

She blinked in surprise.

Kane and Katie returned to the car where Don waited and gave him the rundown.

"Now what?" Don asked as he pulled out of the parking lot into traffic.

"We see if my toys have arrived," Kane said.

When Kane returned to his hotel room twenty minutes later, there was somebody waiting inside.

CHAPTER 11

"Why does General Thurston only call me when there's water involved?"

Kane laughed and shook hands with SEAL Chief Borden Hunt. Codenamed Scimitar, Hunt led his own SEAL team when he wasn't attached to a Team Reaper mission. He and Kane had worked together many times, most notably during the original hunt for Jorge Sanchez and his homicidal daughter, Blanca.

"Because," Kane said, "she knows I can't swim."

"I brought guns and a bunch of the usual crap," Hunt said. He gestured to a trunk sitting on the bed, a steel trunk with leather straps and combination locks. "I call this trunk 'the big case of whoop ass'."

"Could you be a little less obvious?"

"Hey," Hunt said, "the general had to pull a lot of strings to get me in here without getting this trunk checked."

"Did you lug this to the room all by yourself?"

Hunt looked shocked by the question. "Of course."

"How'd you get into my room, by the way?"

The SEAL winked. "That's classified."

Kane shook his head and told Hunt to open the case. Inside, carefully packed, were two well-oiled Heckler & Koch 416 carbines in 5.56mm NATO. Along with an assortment of both 5.56 and 9mm ammunition, the trunk contained tactical vests, communication gear, and six grenades.

"What are those other weapons?"

"Something for your friends, and something we might need against the bad guys."

"Why is it in a zipper case?"

"Because I want it to be a surprise, Reaper. When we plan a party, we bring only the best."

Kane shook his head but allowed Hunt to have his fun.

"What's the score?" Hunt asked.

Kane took a few minutes to explain the situation, starting from the action at the ski village, to the present moment.

"What's your plan?" Hunt asked when Kane finished.

"Hammer party," Kane said. "Tonight."

Ceasario Crisfulli let out a whistle.

"That's a beautiful boat," echoed Bella Lane.

The Evo 43 was docked at the Nassau Marina, and it was an exotic craft. The main feature was the high bow, which made room for copious cabin space below the deck. The deck itself was very spartan, with the cockpit up front surrounded by tinted glass, another section for seating behind the pilot, and the remainder bare wood. The rear deck, at the press of a button, would open wider via hydraulic pumps, and those sections could either extended like wings and remain flat, or be raised several feet to create diving platforms.

Carlos Lorenzo, standing beside Crisfulli and Bella Lane, said, "Plenty of cargo room below the deck, and plenty of power too. This boat will get us in and out of wherever we need to go."

"Let's see inside," Crisfulli said.

The interior cabin had a Plexiglass floor, bunks for sleeping, and a gathering area with circular seating and a table that raised and lowered electronically.

Crisfulli said, "Excellent."

Lorenzo opened a cooler in the right side wall and took out two bottles of beer. Crisfulli and Bella Lane each took one; Lorenzo grabbed a third for himself. They sat on the circular couch. The cabin was well-lighted but had no portholes looking outside, which actually suited Crisfulli just fine.

"I'm nervous about the Brit," Lorenzo said.

"Why?"

"You realize that once word of Bascomb's disappearance gets out, the governor will be obliged to inform the UK that he saw the man here."

"It won't matter by then."

"You changed your mind about killing him?"

"No," Crisfulli said. "I promised I wouldn't as long as he cooperated."

"He'll talk."

"It won't matter."

"Why are you so sure?"

"Because the Americans are doing half of our work for us, right, dear?"

Bella Lane said, "Uh huh," and swallowed some beer.

"How do you know?" Lorenzo asked.

"She's the computer expert, remember?" Crisfulli asked. "We've been tracking their movements in Texas since the disaster in France."

"I wouldn't call it a total disaster," said Bella Lane.

Crisfulli offered her half a smile.

"You're telling me," Lorenzo said, "that you'll be able to go right to the White Wolf's front door, and finish this before anything Bascomb says will be of any use to the police?"

"Yup." Crisfulli drank some beer.

Lorenzo laughed. He took a long drink of beer. Bella Lane sat quietly, legs crossed, beer in her lap, staring at nothing. He looked at Crisfulli.

"When do we start?"

"We need to be ready to leave tonight. Chandler and his men will transport the gear to the boat. I want you to stay here and help them load when they arrive. We'll be at sea overnight."

Lorenzo smiled. "This yacht can take us around the world."

"I'm sure," Crisfulli said. "We only need to cover part of it."

Montenegro
SRETAN CASINO

Cara Billings had to consult Google Translate to learn what "sretan" meant.

"Lucky," she said. "Though it's Croatian, and not Montenegrin."

"Maybe the syndicate was too lazy to learn Montenegrin?" asked Brick as he steered the rented SUV into the parking lot of the sprawling casino and hotel complex. Brick drove, Cara rode shotgun, with Arenas and Traynor in the middle row, and Axe Burton all alone in the very back with only their luggage and gear to keep him company.

"The Croatian language is used here, too," Brick said. "Second most common."

"Wow, somebody's done his homework," Cara said.

"Showoff," Arenas added.

"I've never seen so many cops and soldiers on the street," Traynor added. "You'd think al-Qaeda was here or something."

"You should read the news," Cara told him. "They busted some Russians for trying to overthrow the government last week. Apparently, they didn't want Montenegro joining NATO."

"We miss all the good stuff," Traynor said.

Cara noted that Axe Burton hadn't said much since leaving the airport.

"What's on your mind, Axe?"

"Checkin' out the ladies," Burton said.

Cara rolled her eyes.

Brick circled the large parking lot several times. "Somebody pray for a parking space."

"There," Cara pointed.

Brick slid the large SUV into a too-small space amongst a huge number of cars. They climbed out of the vehicle.

The Sretan Casino had the misfortune of being nowhere near the coast, and thus unable to offer the ocean view so prized by tourists who visited the tiny nation in Southeastern Europe. It sat on the coast of the Adriatic Sea, bordered by Croatia on the western side, with Bosnia and Herzegovina to the northwest. Cara figured the population had a heck of a time during the Balkan Wars of the 1990s. It wasn't fun being smack in the middle of a crossfire.

But the Sretan made an honest attempt to make up for its location. The casino building occupied most of the space, with the hotel adjacent, the hotel stretching into the sky. A "family fun center" also helped attract clientele, with a small water park, and a go-cart racetrack. The go-carts, powered by small motors that sounded to Cara like what one would find on a lawn mower, filled the air. The scent of exhaust fumes tickled her nose.

"Great," she said.

"What's the problem?" Brick asked as he and the other men unloaded the gear.

"The syndicate does its dirty work surrounded by kids."

"No shame," Traynor added.

"Let's get inside," Cara said.

The lobby was opulent, full of marble and crystal, away from the noise of the casino. Cara and her crew checked into several rooms and made their way up the elevator to the 15th floor. Cara told everybody to get settled and join her in her room for the formal briefing. They had no time to waste.

Cara left her suitcase on the bed and opened one of her equipment cases, removing a laptop and a long cable. She plugged one end into the laptop and the other into the wall-mounted flat screen, then tested the connection to make sure what showed on the laptop monitor also appeared on the television. Satisfied, she set about stashing the rest of her gear, the weapons, and her chest rig, in the closet.

When Arenas, Brick, Axe, and Traynor arrived twenty minutes later, they first ordered room service, and while they ate, sat around watching the flat screen.

Cara tapped keys while seated at the writing table and put Desire Cote's picture on the television.

Axe whistled.

"Knock it off," Cara said. But she had to admit Desire Cote was an attractive woman, with long dark hair and dark eyes. The photo was a long shot, taken while she was in public recently, and her yellow sundress looked cute.

"There's our target," she said. "We need to find out if she's working with Ceasario Crisfulli to take over the Corridor."

General Thurston had contacted them during the flight to provide an update on what Kane had learned in Nassau.

"How do you suggest we accomplish this goal?" she asked.

"Make her think Crisfulli is throwing her off the ledge," Traynor said.

"That could work. He tried to get us to kill Caron. Continue."

They kicked around ideas, Burton suggesting he seduce Desire, but with no idea how to go about the rest of the task.

"You're killing me, Axe," Cara said.

Presently they worked out a scenario all agreed with. Carlos suggested cloning her cell phone to listen in on calls and monitor her internet usage. That way, he explained, if they found any trace of communication with Crisfulli, they could get more aggressive with her. If they started by trying to worm their way into her organization, they might find nothing, and waste time. The phone cloning saved time and, if it worked, confirmed they were on the right track.

Cara said, "Now I need a match."

"Why?" Brick asked.

"It's time for the *Mission Impossible* theme."

"I get to be Tom Cruise!" Brick said.

"You can't. You're too big."

"Cruise is too short, but he played Jack Reacher, right?"

Cara considered this a moment. She pressed her lips together in thought. "I'll allow it," she decided.

"Right on!"

"We start with cloning her phone, per Carlos' suggestion," Cara continued. "That means somebody needs to get close to her."

"How close?" Burton asked.

"Not *that* close, Axe."

"Hey," Brick said, "how 'bout I get the female action this time?"

"What's your idea for an approach, Brick?" she asked.

"I'm one hell of a poker player. The intel says she is too. That'll get me close enough for you to clone her phone."

"If she has it on her," Traynor said.

"She'll have it," Cara said. "Everybody's attached to their phones these days. Shouldn't be a problem."

"Don't get caught in the act and captured, Brick," Burton advised. "Billings won't let you forget it."

Cara smiled. She cleared the television screen of Desire Cote's picture.

It felt good to finally be away from headquarters and back in action.

Even with her motley crew of misfits.

Cara and her team weren't the only new arrivals at the Sretan Casino / Hotel.

Adalene Severin landed in Montenegro with the mercenary named Voltaire and didn't bother with a phony passport. She was not wanted anywhere in the world. Her name would trip no alarms. Such was the benefit of working closely with the White Wolf and keeping her activities on the down low.

Voltaire, however, traveled under an alias: Victor Hansen. She wondered if it were anything close to his real name.

They checked into separate rooms, but their plan was already fully formed, and there was nothing else to discuss.

Spring cleaning, yeah.

They were there to kill Desire Cote.

With extreme prejudice.

Nassau

Bad things happen when the sun goes down.

When Ceasario Crisfulli and Bella Lane arrived at the marina, Carlos Lorenzo had all the equipment loaded, and Brad Chandler and Rosen, the mercenaries, were ready to depart.

Jackson, the third merc, remained at the villa to guard Leland Bascomb. The Brit's job was done; Crisfulli planned to release him upon their return, put him on a plane back to London, and carry on his with his agenda.

Lorenzo continued to advocate that they kill Bascomb, but Crisfulli flatly refused. He understood where Carlos was coming from, but Crisfulli's fight was not with Bascomb, or anybody else, other than Team Reaper, if they interfered and he still had plans for the anti-drug strike force. Bella Lane confirmed their arrival in Montenegro, thanks to informants at the casino, so Crisfulli knew they were still on the hook. It also meant they were nowhere near Nassau.

However, the identities of the three Americans in Nassau

that Carlos had mentioned remained a mystery. They might be members of Reaper, but his informants confirmed five people at the casino, and that matched the amount who'd gone after Aymard Caron, so perhaps the trio were CIA. If that was the case, they might need to be disabled, but Crisfulli was confident that he could easily evade them instead. He really didn't have the time for a protracted counter-mission. If the White Wolf was aware of his impending doom, Crisfulli had more pressing matters to deal with. His vengeance would not be denied. That was the goal.

Crisfulli and Bella Lane went below while Lorenzo started the motors and steered the Evo out of the dock. Chandler and Rosen remained above with Lorenzo, running last-minute checks on their gear and the underwater drone. Two hours to target.

Crisfulli helped himself to a beer and handed one to Bella. She snapped off the top.

He sat beside her.

"Almost done, my dear."

"Did I ever tell you," she said, "that I don't necessarily approve of you still pining for an old girlfriend."

"I'm not pining for an old girlfriend," he said. "I am avenging an old girlfriend."

"Same thing."

"It's not."

Crisfulli sighed and said nothing, letting the drone of the engines fill the silence. But Bella Lane stared at him. She expected an explanation, and he had to admit he'd never provided one.

"I was a young man," he said. "I'd worked my way from the Union Corse into the Corridor, just like the White Wolf. I was in love with a young lady named Ariana, we were going to get married, but the Wolf took a liking to her too."

"He stole her from you?"

"He tried. When she didn't succumb to his charms, he had her killed."

"You have proof?"

"It was supposed to have been an accident. A car wreck late at night on a busy motorway in Milan. Police never found the driver. Neither did I. It was the perfect hit."

"But you stayed in the syndicate? Why?"

"I pretended to believe the story. The Wolf was sympathetic. He put me in a higher position. And that's when I started planning my revenge."

"You were smart enough not to steal his money, too."

"He'd have known something was up if I'd dipped into the coffers. Instead, my planning consisted of learning everything about him, his hideouts, false identities, everything," Crisfulli said. "There is nowhere he can run where I can't find him. I only needed money to assemble a crew to make the final assault."

"Chandler and his mercenaries."

"Correct."

"How long have you been waiting?"

"Fifteen years."

"You have the patience of a saint."

"Or a sniper." Crisfulli drank some beer. "That's why we must remain focused and not let petty details derail our plans."

"The Americans."

"Team Reaper will come in handy, and when they're done, I shall dispose of them as I'll dispose of the Wolf. I haven't told you that part of the plan."

She smiled. "I'm sure it's a good one."

"There's a reason I've had you monitor their headquarters. Team Reaper will be a thing of the past, and nothing will stand in our way once we're in charge."

"I like how you say we."

"I can't do it without you, babe."

"I better not step out of line," she said.

"You'll get the spanking of your life if you do," he said.

"Maybe I'll step out of line just a little," she said, then grinned.

"I'll paddle your bottom until it's red."

"You should do that anyway. Make it so I can't sit for a week."

This time, Crisfulli smiled.

"What about his woman?"

"Severin? She's not his woman."

"His favorite killer then."

"She prefers to kill by proxy when she can," Crisfulli said. "She'll supervise but let somebody else pull the trigger. Except when she doesn't, of course."

"To revenge," Bella Lane said, extending her bottle.

Crisfulli clinked his with hers. They drank.

The beer tasted really good.

Waves crashed ferociously against the seawall.

The tides had become aggressive with nightfall, the full moon in the sky the only witness to the motorboat approaching Crisfulli's villa.

Don Mateo sat behind the wheel of the 21-inch Malibu TXI. He wore all black, including a black cap on his head, his face streaked with black combat cosmetics.

Behind him, crouched low, were John Kane and SEAL Chief Borden Hunt.

They'd chosen to rent the Malibu because it was large enough, and had enough seating, in case Leland Bascomb was in bad shape and needed space to lay down. Two seats were set behind the cockpit glass, Don at the controls, Kane beside him. Hunt sat in the back, behind Kane, with some narrow deck space between the engine hump in the center. The forward seating area ahead of the cockpit, allowing enough space for somebody to lay flat, provided needed defensive space.

Katie remained at the hotel, standing by. There had been no further sign of Lorenzo or Crisfulli at the resort, however.

Which meant they were either at the villa or already at sea going for the Sanchez money.

Kane and Hunt would do the dirty work of raiding the villa. Don had not liked the arrangement.

"Why do you two get to have all the fun?" he asked.

"I'm trying to keep you alive. You have a wife to think about," Kane had told him. "Just drive the boat and leave the shooting to us."

"You're going to leave me in the boat without a weapon?"

"Of course not," Kane had replied. The trunk Hunt had brought contained two extra weapons, one each for Katie and Don. As he drove the Malibu, a Russian SR-1 Veresk, chosen because it couldn't be linked to the US, rode across his back. The crudely designed submachine gun chambered the blunt nosed yet potent 9x21mm Gyurza cartridge.

"Defensive use only," Kane had advised. "Let us do the hard stuff."

Don had grumbled but agreed.

He steered the motorboat over the rocky waves, the seawall in sight. The villa was partially lit inside, indicating somebody was still there. If they could get the British ocean explorer free of his captors, then settle accounts with Crisfulli and Lorenzo, their mission in Nassau would be complete and give the rest of Team Reaper in Montenegro a free hand.

General Thurston had called prior to their departure with an update.

"We've been in touch with MI5 in London," she'd said. "They've moved on the house where Mrs. Bascomb was being held. She's free. Two men in custody."

"Have they told us anything useful?"

"Not yet, but we might not require them. They'll be kept in reserve in case we need to put some pressure on."

"All right," Kane had said.

"Good luck, Reaper."

"Thank you, ma'am."

Kane checked his HK 416 as Don cut the motor and let the waves carry them the rest of the way to the seawall. When the motorboat bumped against the edge of the wall, Kane and Hunt jumped out of the boat in a flash. Both put one hand on the top of the wall and vaulted over. In an instant, they were gone. Don Mateo threw a rope around a rock outcropping to anchor the boat and unslung the Veresk. He sat with the weapon in hand. Waves pushed at the boat and the forward hull bumped against the seawall.

Kane and Hunt landed on soft grass. Dropping low, they scanned the yard. No sign of dogs or foot patrols.

"How many you think are in there?" Hunt asked.

"The cleaning lady said three, plus the hostage."

"Palm trees make decent cover."

"Split up," Kane said.

Kane left first, crossing left diagonally to a palm tree about fifteen yards away. He dropped to one knee and swept his HK left and right, catching Hunt's movement in his peripheral vision. Kane moved again, cutting right this time, and stopped at another palm. He was close enough to see through the windows, especially the lit area, but spotted no movement. He followed the line of dark windows. The bedrooms behind those windows would not, according to Francesca, the cleaning lady, contain Bascomb. She'd also noticed no wires around the windows or glass, which meant they hadn't set up any explosives to counteract a breach. Kane had a glass cutter in his pack and entering the house through one of the bedrooms might be better than a direct assault on the living room.

Kane looked across at Hunt, tapping two fingers on his upper right forearm. Hunt separated from the palm and moved quickly through the open space to join Kane.

"I'm going for that bedroom window," Kane said.

"A grenade at the patio window might distract everybody while you do that."

"Don't miss."

Kane left the palm and sprinted to the side of the house, dropping below the darkened window. There was a curtain across the glass on the other side. Kane felt around the outer windowsill, found no wires there either. Slinging his HK, he removed the glass cutter from a side pouch. Placing the suction cup on the glass, he began rotating the blade. It screeched on the glass. Kane paused, grateful for the soundtrack of the crashing waves to cover the noise. He continued moving the blade. Pretty soon it wouldn't matter how loud he was.

He didn't watch Hunt toss his fragmentation grenade. The pineapple announced its presence all by itself.

The blast shook the ground and the house. Kane felt the window vibrate. He swung the cutter sharply, removing the suction cup, which took away a perfect circle of glass. Shoving his gloved left hand through the hole, Kane found the catch. He flicked it up and pulled the window open about four inches. With his Ka-Bar Marine knife, he slashed the mesh screen, shoving the window open the rest of the way.

Gunfire. Single shots, popping rapidly. They weren't the light pops of the 5.56mm tumblers chambered in the Heckler & Koch 416 carbine; they were heavier. And only one gun.

Kane wondered how large a force they faced inside. Or was it only one man? One guard for the captured Leland Bascomb?

If so, it meant the others had already left to find the Sanchez money.

Kane cursed as he slid his body through the open window, tumbling onto the carpet inside. The bedroom appeared well-furnished, but he didn't stop to admire the bedspread. Moving quickly to the closed door, he opened it a crack and looked into the empty hallway.

The shooting continued, growing more intense. Hunt had joined in; the light pops of his 5.56mm rounds unmistakable.

Then the gunfire ceased.

"Scimitar, Reaper One."

Hunt's voice over the com unit.

"Reaper One, go," Kane whispered.

"There's only one guy! He knocked over a table for cover."

"Copy, one shooter. I'm inside."

Kane slipped into the hallway, keeping close to the door. He heard a man's voice.

quickly slapped another into the weapon, but there was no need for another blast.

"Reaper One to Scimitar."

"Go."

"Water's warm. I'm going for Bascomb."

"Coming to you."

Kane charged down the hall once again. *Last room on the right.* He stopped at the bedroom door.

"Leland Bascomb! Can you hear me?"

The reply was faint, tinged with fear, but the Brit responded.

"I hear you!"

Kane tested the doorknob. Locked, of course.

"You're being rescued, step away from the door."

Kane moved back and launched a hard kick into the door, once, twice. Third time was the charm. The door swung inward, crashing against the opposite wall. Kane charged through the doorway. He swung his weapon left, right, no threats. The only person in the room was Leland Bascomb, shackled at wrists and ankles, and laying on the carpet.

Kane slung the HK across his back and knelt before the hostage.

"My family!" the British ocean explorer said. His eyes were wide with fear, face coated with sweat.

"Mr. Bascomb, listen to me carefully. Your family is safe. They are with MI5 in London."

Bascomb's shoulders sank a little as stress deflated from his body. Kane examined the shackles. Steel cuffs.

"I'm going for the key."

Bascomb nodded. Kane raced back to the living room, finding Hunt there near the body of the dead mercenary.

"Nice shooting," Hunt said.

"Hostage down the hall. Check that guy for a key."

Kane turned his back to Hunt and maintained a danger scan. They couldn't relax for one second.

"Got it."

Kane took the key from Hunt's gloved hand. The key was smeared with blood. Luckily, the blood didn't belong to Kane or Hunt.

Kane ran back to Bascomb and unlocked the wrist and ankle cuffs. Bascomb jumped to his feet.

"Where are the others?" Kane asked.

"Gone! They left a few hours ago." He added, "At least I think it was a few hours."

"You're sure they're gone?"

"Yes! They're going for the money."

"Do you know where?"

"Look at the map. The map!"

"Show me the map. We gotta move fast."

Bascomb took the lead, running down the hall to the living room once again, where the wall map with the hand-drawn X still hung. Kane looked at the spot but had to admit it was meaningless.

"Can you get to this place?" Kane asked the Brit.

"All I need is a boat."

"We have a boat," Kane said. "Can you run?"

"Around the world, if necessary."

"Let's go. Hunt, on our six."

"Copy!" Hunt shouted.

Kane and Bascomb ran through the patio doors first, Hunt a few feet behind. They ran straight for the seawall and didn't look back.

CHAPTER 12

Montenegro
SRETAN CASINO

At six-foot-three with his shaved head and tattoos, Richard "Brick" Peters seemed to dwarf everybody in the casino.

Even at the noon hour, the casino was packed with players, mostly at the slot machines, but the roulette wheels, crap games, and poker tables were doing tremendous business. They knew from Desire Cote's background that she liked playing poker, five card stud specifically, not the awful Texas Hold-'em, aka *The Game That Killed Poker*. Ever since that stupid movie from the 1990s with the too-young actor who wanted everybody to think he was an expert card player, every man in America dragged their Dad Bods to the card tables and didn't know other versions of poker existed, and, worse, refused to learn, because "it wasn't in dat movie, bro". Desire Cote might be a slimy drug thug worthy of a bullet, but Brick admired her adherence to traditional poker. The *best* poker.

Brick found her at a corner table, taking on the suckers.

The table was a mix of nationalities, but all tourists, and while they might have been good at their neighborhood poker games, they were no match for Desire's smoldering eyes and a straight face that gave away nothing. The pile of chips in front of her testified to how much she'd already taken off the men seated at her table who were simply no match.

Brick smiled. He didn't just *play* poker; he *loved* poker. He wasn't dumb enough to play online, either. One only excelled at such a game when dealing with people face-to-face. He might lose to the woman, but he had a better chance of cleaning her out than the assembled chumps at the table.

But he smiled as he waited for a seat. This time, the game wasn't about winning. This time, he had a different goal. He was still going to clean Desire Cote out, but he wouldn't be touching her money. Well, most of it.

The wait wasn't long. At the conclusion of yet another hand won by Desire Cote, several suckers decided they'd had enough and excused themselves. Two brave souls remained. Brick pulled out a chair, and the dealer told him the buy-in. Brick covered the amount with cash, and the dealer passed him a stack of chips, which he kept before him, the reds, whites, and blues neatly arranged.

Desire Cote gave him a wry smile.

He smiled back.

She wore a simple white blouse and blue jeans combo, no jewelry, only a little make-up. Nothing about her appearance or attire suggested who she really was. She'd tied back her long hair, and neither she nor Brick acknowledged each other verbally. He did notice how she dropped her eyes to her stack of chips. *Am I making you nervous, dear?*

"The game is five card stud," the dealer announced, as she shuffled cards. She offered Brick the break. He took off the top half and set it beside the other, and the dealer put the stacks together and gave one final shuffle. The dealer was another woman, dressed in the white blouse, black slacks, and black vest of all the female casino employees. Very quickly, the dealer snapped cards to each player, and presently, Brick looked at his five cards. Two of the tourists had the first blind bets, and Brick kept his eyes low, and his cards close as play began.

He wore no jacket, as the interior environment of the casino gave him no need for one. The cell phone in his right pants pocket, however, was on and waiting for the magic to happen. He was close enough to Desire Cote that Cara Billings, back in her room and guided by Sam Swift at head-quarters, that cloning Cote's cell phone would be a simple process.

The goal was to make a copy of Desire Cote's phone without physically touching the device. To somebody like Brick, who knew the basics of everyday tech but nothing more complicated, it seemed like an impossible task. *Cue the theme, Cara.* But Sam "Slick" Swift, the red-headed hacker at headquarters, knew a lot more than Brick and said the process was so simple, a child could accomplish the task. Brick wasn't sure about that, but he trusted Slick, and Cara was convinced, too. Brick's job was to get close to Desire Cote. Done. He couldn't get closer, at the moment, than across from her at a poker table. Now he was supposed to sit and play cards. That was easy. He also wasn't allowed to touch the phone in his pocket. No problem. Brick wasn't allowed to touch the phone in his pocket, because Slick and Cara needed control of the functions. And that's where Brick checked out. Their side of the operation was above his pay grade and something he had no desire to learn. As the team medic, he had his own specialized knowledge, and he was happy to leave the geek stuff to the people who truly enjoyed that subject.

The phone in Brick's pocket contained the usual contact list, applications, and other nonsense should some-body get a close look at the phone. That same person would even find Angry Birds and various other silly games that Brick insisted be added for color. What that close look wouldn't reveal was what hid beneath the façade.

The phone contained a Bluetooth-based hacking tool developed by Sam Swift. The red-headed hacker had explained that there were several similar tools available to the public if one knew where to look, but he wasn't happy with those, so he developed his own tool.

Brick sat and played cards, betting, checking, raising, and all the while, a part of him was wondering what the allegedly silent cell phone in his pocket was doing.

"Tell me what you see," said Swift via the secure cell connection with headquarters. Cara Billings, seated at the desk in her hotel room, had Swift on speakerphone. Pete Traynor stood behind her, watching over her shoulder.

Brick was downstairs doing his poker thing, but he wasn't entirely alone. She'd told Arenas and Axe to roam the casino and keep an eye on Brick. Just in case. Brick wasn't armed, but that didn't mean he was weak. Still, if the worst happened, she wanted the Team Reaper big man and trained medic to have back-up. It was the same reason she had Traynor with her. Just in case.

"I have my laptop connected to Brick's phone, and I can see the list of Bluetooth devices near him."

"Jackson to Chandler, emergency. We're under attack, do you copy?"

How far away was the rest of the crew? If they were already at sea, poor Jackson was on his own. If they had left only a few minutes prior, they might have time to turn back.

The numbers started falling fast in Kane's head.

Move. Now!

Kane jammed the HK into his shoulder and advanced down the hall.

"Jackson to Chandler, do you copy?"

Poor bastard. There'd be no backup tonight. Kane flicked the HK's selector switch from semi- to full-auto.

"Reaper One to Scimitar."

"Go."

"Hold your fire."

"Copy."

Kane cleared the hallway and entered the wide living room, swinging right. Cold air from outside blasted his face, the wrecked patio doors exposing the interior to the outer elements. The lone defender had turned over a dining table for cover, the thick wood having stopped Hunt's salvos. The lone merc crouched low with an FN-FAL in both hands, the weapons 7.62mm NATO rounds certainly more powerful than the HK, but only if Kane missed.

Jackson turned quickly, but not fast enough. As the long snout of the FN zeroed on Kane, Reaper One let a full-auto burst flash from his HK.

The rounds stitched Jackson shoulder to neck, punching through and smashing into the underside of the table. Jackson's body thudded against the wood, Kane letting off the trigger to step closer. He paused with a couch between him and his target, and fired again, emptying the magazine into the mercenary. He dropped the mag and

"You should see Cote's at the top of the list."

Cara read the device name. "MissDesire01?"

"Why do they make it so obvious?"

"Because they never think we're sneaking up their backside," Cara said. "What do you want me to do?"

"Click on it."

Cara positioned the mouse pointer over *MissDesire01* and clicked.

"Now what?"

"This is the good part," Swift said, his giddiness unmistakable. "Don't touch anything."

A blue bar beneath the *MissDesire01* entry began moving left to right.

"What's happening?" Cara asked. "Please explain to the little people."

"You know how you download files from the internet? Or email attachments, things like that?"

"Sure."

"That's what we're doing here, except we're downloading Cote's entire phone, basically copying the operating system, which will give us her contacts, search history, recent calls, the whole shebang."

"How is this possible?"

"Every cell phone has certain vulnerabilities that people like me can exploit," Slick said. "No tech security is foolproof. My tool finds those weaknesses and slips through the holes the same way somebody like you cuts through a security fence. Get it?"

"Sure," Cara said. *Almost.*

"My program then makes a copy of the software on her phone. Cell phones are small computers, but nobody treats them that way."

"And Bluetooth is your trojan horse?"

"If they only knew!" Slick laughed. "Best hacking tool ever. Why do you think cell phones aren't allowed on military bases, especially in classified areas? Anybody at the CIA being caught with a phone inside the building can be fired. Phones can be hacked and used as listening devices; you can activate the camera and capture footage, all kinds of things. They're actually quite dangerous to people like us."

Cara glanced at Traynor, who shrugged.

"I'll smash mine with a hammer at the next opportunity," Cara said.

"Where's the blue bar?" Swift asked.

"Almost all the way across. What if something interferes with the transmission?"

"It will automatically try again, as long as Brick remains close to the target."

"Which means," Traynor said, finally speaking up, "if we get interference, Brick better not run out of money."

"Never mind that," Cara said. "He better not clean Miss Desire out of *her* money. Because then she'll leave the table. I can't imagine she'd want to *then* have a conversation with the fellow who wiped out her cash, even if he's big and good-looking."

"You noticed?" Traynor asked. The former DEA man had a grin like he'd caught Cara with her hand in the cookie jar.

Cara glared at him.

Nassau

Ceasario Crisfulli was too excited to sit below deck and wait.

Brad Chandler, the mercenary captain, kept his eye on a portable GPS unit as Carlos Lorenzo steered the yacht. The night was cold, the sea rough, but the sight before them was beautiful. There was something mystical about the open ocean, especially at night, when only the moon lit the way, casting a knife edge of light across the surface of the water.

"Left two degrees and hold steady," Chandler said, not looking up from the glowing screen of the GPS unit. Lorenzo turned the wheel slightly, watching the instrument panel, and then turned the boat straight once again.

"Should have them in sight," Chandler added, finally looking up.

Crisfulli followed his gaze and smiled. There they were, just like Bascomb had described. A rocky formation forming three peaks, with a string of caves beneath.

"How close can we get?" Crisfulli asked.

"As close as the rocks will let us," Lorenzo said.

Chandler handed the GPS unit to Crisfulli and moved to the rear deck, where Rosen waited with the dive gear and the underwater drone. Crisfulli glanced back. They were preparing the drone for its remote dive prior to donning their SCUBA gear. Crisfulli had agreed that it would be best to check the site remotely prior to sending them down. He was excited but didn't deny the butterflies in his gut. His entire plan was riding on the money being there, the map being real, this whole exercise being more than a waste of time and effort.

But what if it was wasted? The process had begun. The White Wolf and his minions knew what was going on, Caron was probably already dead, with Desire Cote next on the Wolf's death list. Crisfulli might not be able to afford Chandler and the rest of his troops after tonight, but nothing could stop him now. There was no turning back, no matter how the cave search turned out.

It took another ten minutes, and then Lorenzo cut the engines. The Evo 43 drifted to the rocks, bumping against the side.

"Do be careful," Crisfulli said. "This is an expensive boat."

Lorenzo ignored the remark and pressed a button on the console before him. A motor at the front of the yacht whirred to life and presently stopped.

"Anchor down," Lorenzo said.

Crisfulli went below and told Bella Lane that she didn't want to miss the search. She left the galley couch reluctantly, pulling on a heavy coat as she followed Crisfulli back up top.

Chandler and Rosen had the drone prepared. Rosen set the craft in the water, where it immediately washed under the surface. Rosen then pulled a box from his utility belt, extending an antenna, and placing his thumbs on the control modules on either side. Crisfulli frowned. He hadn't expected the remote unit to resemble the same type used to operate a remote-controlled airplane or car, but why not? Chandler adjusted the brightness on the small laptop he held, and the display filled with the darkness of the ocean below. Rosen flipped a switch. The laptop screen lit up. A haze of clear blue, some particles visible in the headlight beam, appeared on the monitor, along with text information displaying speed, depth, and other pertinent information Crisfulli expected Chandler understood quite well.

"My butt is freezing," Bella Lane said.

Crisfulli ignored her. The cold didn't affect him any longer. His body was flush with heat, with the anticipation of discovery.

Rosen pressed forward on one of the control modules, and the underwater drone began its travel to the caves below the surface, the movement reflected on the laptop monitor, the information on screen communicating to the silent Chandler as he concentrated on the task.

The yacht drifted up and down on the ocean surface.

"Won't be long now," Chandler said, as Rosen, using the laptop for reference, steered the drone into the mouth of the first cave below. The headlamp brightness intensified as the close quarters of the cave walls intensified the beam, but all they saw on the screen was a dark circle ahead and the 360-degree jagged cave walls.

"How much room would we have there?" Chandler asked.

"Not enough," Rosen replied. "I don't think this is the one."

"Go all the way to the end," Crisfulli ordered.

Chandler and Rosen made no reply as Rosen continued steering the drone. The cave curved slightly left, finally ending at a rock wall.

"Back up," Chandler said.

"In progress." Rosen worked the controls, and they stood for another few minutes watching the monitor image travel in reverse.

When the drone cleared the first cave, Rosen aimed for the next opening, this one larger than the first, the walls equally jagged, but both Chandler and Rosen agreed that traveling down the length of the second cave was more than feasible. Maybe they were close to the hidden money, though there were still plenty of nooks they might need to look within.

They might be at sea all night.

· · ·

"You busted my streak," Desire Cote said. "At least buy a girl a drink."

Brick frowned. "You're the first person I've beaten at poker," he said, "that didn't want to come at me with a machete and told me so."

"Night's still young," Desire said.

Brick laughed.

The hand in question hadn't been particularly spectacular. Brick had played for several hours, winning and losing in equal turn, his stack never dropping to the point of obvious distress. The same could be said of Desire Cote's playing. Her eyes flashed a certain level of excitement when he placed a bet. He challenged her, and she enjoyed the challenge. She did not get that look when one of the tourists placed a bet.

After playing for almost three hours, Brick decided it was time to stop. He'd gone longer than Cara told him would be required because he was enjoying the challenge too.

Finally, he went all in on three jacks and two aces.

The bold move chased out the tourists, who folded.

Desire Cote bit her lower lip as she considered her next move. Meanwhile, Brick stared at her with unblinking eyes.

Desire Cote called the bet but lost with her four of a kind.

Brick collected the chips, tipped the dealer, and quietly left the table. He felt Desire Cote's eyes on him all the way out of the casino.

Brick cashed the chips, having the money deposited onto a pre-paid debit card, and proceeded to the bar. He'd be lying if he said his pulse wasn't racing, his mind spinning from the win. He'd won big pots before, but never against somebody who, if she wanted, could snap her fingers and have a guy whack him before bedtime.

As Desire Cote looked at him while he sipped a vodka tonic with lime, he gestured to the bartender.

"Whatever the lady wants," he said.

"Cosmo."

The bartender nodded.

Brick said, "Sit down if you'd like."

She perched on the stool next to him, facing Brick directly. He turned to face her.

"Who are you?"

"Call me Brick," he said.

"Because of your size?"

"Because of my muscle mass." He laughed.

She shook her head but was laughing with her eyes. "That wasn't a normal poker game, was it?"

"What do you mean?"

"What do you want, Mr. Brick? Why are you here?"

"Vacation. Playing cards." He shrugged. "I'm not sure what else you mean."

"You're no tourist."

Brick said, "You seem to know. Why don't you tell me what I am?"

Desire Cote's eyes moved up and down Brick's chest. Her eyes felt like an x-ray. He tried not to sweat.

"You're a soldier."

"Maybe."

"What else could you be? Look at the men in this place. Nobody has your physique."

"Are you projecting your desires on me?"

She laughed. "Hardly." She leaned close. "You weren't playing poker. You were trying to get my attention. Why?"

"You tell me."

"Because you know who I am, and you want a job."

"A job doing what?"

She pulled away, laughing again. "Maybe I'm wrong. Perhaps you're with the European Narcotics Bureau."

"Not with my record."

"What kind of record is that?"

"Let's say you might be right about one or two things."

"Which two?"

"I'm not a tourist. I *am* a soldier."

"What kind?"

"The kind that's between jobs right now."

"There are plenty of soldiers looking for work. I have too many of them on my payroll as it is."

"I'm also a trained medic."

"I have a few of those, too."

"I guess we're done here."

"Thanks for the drink, Mr. Brick. And good luck on your job search. Next time, don't steal your potential boss's lunch money."

This time Brick laughed. She left the bar without looking back.

Brick finished his drink, and the ice clinked as he placed the empty glass on the bar.

He hoped he kept her talking long enough for Cara to have extra time with the phone trick. He had no way of knowing what their status was. He left the barstool and a tip for the bartender. Time to get back to Cara and the others and see if the mission had been successful, or a complete waste of a perfectly good night.

But at least he'd be taking home some extra spending money. Wasn't all bad.

. . .

"Eyes on target," said the mercenary named Voltaire.

"Terminate," said Adalene Severin.

She watched Desire Cote leave the main building and travel across the courtyard to a cluster of small buildings where she kept her office. All the doors were marked Private, and if that wasn't enough, a small fence, about waist-level to the average person, circled the cluster too. You needed a key card to pass through the gate. Desire Cote didn't travel with a bodyguard. It was a common fault with members of the Corridor, Adalene had noticed, and more than once. They thought they were invincible because they had the White Wolf on their side. In this case, the thought could not have been more incorrect.

But a bodyguard wouldn't have saved her, anyway. A bodyguard would have been yet another body for the police to dispose of.

With only Desire Cote laying on the ground, they wouldn't have to work as hard.

Adalene figured they'd appreciate that. Cops were overworked and underappreciated as it was. The least she could do was not leave more than one corpse lying around.

She said, "Target almost to the fence." She stood near a support post in the open-air food area, which was quite crowded despite the cool night, but the temperature was helped by strategically placed space heaters, which kept the customers happy.

No response from Voltaire. He was ignoring her. It was his way of telling her to shut her mouth and let him do the job she'd hired him for. She took the silent rebuke stoically. He had a point. She could have done the job herself. No question about that. But part of her strategy for staying off the radar required letting others do the actual work, while she directed from stage left.

Adalene still wasn't used to the com unit's earpiece, which, to her, felt like it was sticking so far out of her ear that passersby not only would see it but know what she was using it for. Luckily, the sensitivity of the unit allowed her to keep her voice down while being loud and clear for Voltaire.

The mercenary, with a scoped rifle, was somewhere off the property but with a perfect view of the intended field of fire. Desire didn't vary her routine much, and it was only a matter of time before she crossed through the magnified scope.

Adalene looked at her nails. She'd had them repainted, and the bright red looked good. The nails matched her lipstick. Under the overcoat, which protected her from the evening's chill, was a matching red minidress. If this had been a normal night, she'd have had men lined up for blocks to spend even five minutes with her, if her pale white skin didn't clash with the dress and make her look like a deformed candy cane.

She'd told Voltaire not to use a suppressor on his rifle. She wanted to hear the shot and see Desire Cote's body fall. It would be tragic if the woman was not a traitor, but it was a chance they couldn't take, and if the Wolf said she needed to die, it wasn't Adalene's place to argue. She only had to watch her back just in case the Wolf had put her on the death list, too.

The shot cracked across the property, swallowed only by the kiddie area and the loud bumper cars.

"Target down."

"I see her," Adalene said. "Flat on her back."

"See you at the rendezvous."

"Copy, good job."

. . .

Cara was still on the speakerphone with Sam Swift back in Texas, scrolling through a furious amount of information on her laptop.

But the rifle shot reached their ears anyway.

"Who's firing?" she asked.

Traynor went to the window, carefully parting the curtains, opening enough of a gap to see outside.

"Can't tell from here."

"I hope it's not what I think it is," Cara said.

"I'll go find Brick."

Traynor left the room in a hurry.

Cara Billings keyed her com unit to reach Arenas and Axe. They responded.

"What's happening?"

"Shooting near the outdoor food court," Axe replied. "One shot, one person down."

"Who?"

"Who do you *think*, Reaper Two? It's Desire Cote. She fell like a chopped tree."

Cara drummed her fingers on the tabletop where the computer sat. Luckily, they had everything they needed, but a dead woman's cell phone had finite value.

"Reaper Three and Four, stay and observe," she ordered.

"Copy," Axe said.

"HQ," Cara said, "do you copy?"

General Thurston came over the speaker. "Copy, Desire down. Any sign of life?"

"Apparently not. Slick?"

"I'm cataloging her phone records and internet activity right now," the hacker said. "Won't take more than a few minutes."

"We need to dig, Slick."

"Way ahead of you."

"Reaper Two," the general said, "it's safe to say you're done there, but I want you to remain on location. Whatever Slick finds, it'll be on your side of the world. There's no sense coming home."

"As long as there's somewhere to *go*, we don't mind," Cara said.

"We'll have something. One way or another. We have two of Crisfulli's people on ice in London. Worse case, we interrogate."

"As long as the Brits cooperate, ma'am."

"I'm aware of the challenges, Reaper Two. Stand by."

Thurston clicked off the air.

Cara Billings stared at the laptop screen, which Slick was connected to, and watched the information displayed download to a folder on his side.

She hoped the data proved useful.

Because either Ceasario Crisfulli or the White Wolf was cleaning house, and Team Reaper faced the possibility of being cut out of the final showdown unless Kane and his friends in Nassau succeeded in cutting Crisfulli off at the pass.

Nassau

Third time's the charm.

The drone entered the third cave under the ocean, this one also wide, perhaps wider than the second option. Crisfulli watched the laptop screen with the increasing anticipation of finally scoring the prize. The biting cold no longer bothered him, though Bella Lane had gone below after the second cave proved a bust. If she wanted to miss the grand finale, that was her business.

The wind picked up a little more, chilling Crisfulli from neck to feet. But his eyes did not leave the computer monitor as Rosen steered the drone along the length of the cave, the bright headlamp lighting the way.

"Right there," Rosen said, quietly.

Crisfulli pushed past Chandler to look closer.

No doubt.

A black steel container sat in front of the drone camera, growing in size as the drone approached. It had been placed without any thought of concealment. The money *was* meant to be picked up eventually, after all.

"Time for a dive, Rosen," Chandler said.

Rosen closed the laptop and placed it on the deck. Crisfulli hurried to re-open it and carried it below to show Bella.

On the deck, Chandler and Rosen quickly donned their diving equipment. They were already wearing wet suits. Sitting on the gunwale while they secured their flippers, the two men did a final check on their air supply and then tipped over the side. They splashed into the water.

Crisfulli let out a cry of excitement as he dropped onto the couch beside Bella Lane, who was working on another glass of wine and looked a little glassy around the eyes. They stared at the unmoving container for what seemed like an eternity.

"Why didn't they pull the drone out first?" Bella Lane asked.

"They need the light," Crisfulli told her, his eyes fixed on the image.

All of it was coming together. He had no dream of

conquest, per se, but he did dream of revenge, revenge against the man who took away somebody he loved because *that man* had insatiable visions of conquest and it didn't matter what stood in his way. Now, with the Sanchez money in his possession, Crisfulli could hire more mercenaries, and his assault on the den of the White Wolf would culminate in his long-held desire to have the Wolf at the end of a gun.

The coming victory tasted sweet on his tongue.

Chandler and Rosen appeared on the screen display, each with plenty of room in the cave. They were side-by-side as they started to drag the case from its hiding spot. The jostling of the water around them shook the drone, the camera tipping down and away from the shot.

Crisfulli grinned.

Only a few more minutes.

What helped, when Chandler and Rosen finally pulled the case from the mouth of the cave, was the flotation unit on the bottom of the case. Chandler noticed it first as they bent to lift the case. He had to pull a pin, and the cushion at the bottom inflated. The case began to float to the top. Chandler and Rosen rushed to keep up with the case. They were at a depth where the bends wasn't an issue, so they swam quickly, grabbing the case by the side handles and swimming back to the surface.

Once they broke water, however, they needed Carlos Lorenzo to help pull the case over the gunwale while they pushed. Lorenzo lost his balance and fell onto the deck with a grunt, but the case was on board the boat.

Lorenzo was on his feet, brushing off his clothes when Crisfulli emerged onto the deck. Chandler and Rosen climbed aboard, dripping wet. It took a few minutes to get their gear off. When they did, still in their wetsuits, the four men examined the steel case and the locks holding the lid closed.

"Combo locks," Chandler said.

Crisfulli pulled a piece of paper from the pockets of his pants, one of the pieces of paper recovered from the lockbox taken from Mexico. A series of numbers had been jotted on the paper, and they could only be the codes for the combination locks that seemed to stump Chandler.

The boat rocked on the water, the wind unrelenting, as Crisfulli turned the tumblers of each of the three combo locks. He didn't snap them open upon completion. He wanted to open all three at the same time. His pulse was racing, his hand shaking — and not from the cold. Adrenaline poured through his system. This was it. This was the end of one quest and the beginning of another.

With the last combination entered, Crisfulli flicked his thumb over the switches in quick succession. One, two, three, each lock popped, and nobody interfered with him lifting the steel lid.

Lorenzo said, "Mother of mercy."

"Wow," Chandler said.

Rosen added, "I thought this whole thing was fake."

"Yee of little faith," Crisfulli said, as his dark eyes took in the stacked American greenbacks filling the case.

He quickly closed the lid. "We have to secure this. It's going to be a bumpy ride home."

Chandler and Rosen grabbed ropes to tie the case down.

Crisfulli turned to Lorenzo. "How fast can you get us home?"

"How fast do you want to go?" Lorenzo asked.

Crisfulli smiled and slapped his friend on the back. Then he laughed. The sound of his laugh carried in the wind.

CHAPTER 13

"Radar is picking up another boat," Carlos Lorenzo said.

Ceasario Crisfulli stepped beside the other man, who sat at the Evo 43 controls, which included a small radar screen on the facing console. He ignored the spray of water splashing over the bow as the boat bounced on the rough water, but held true to the set course. He had asked Lorenzo to head for Nassau at the best possible speed.

"All I see is a white dot," Crisfulli said.

"Indicators on the gauge below. It's another boat, not traveling as fast as us, but heading in our direction."

Crisfulli went below, where he found Chandler and the others and asked Chandler to get Jackson on the radio. His excitement was turning to dread; if somebody had raided the villa, they had seen the map, they knew what Crisfulli was looking for, and now they'd have to shoot their way out of Nassau. This was exactly what he'd hoped to avoid. His only question was whether or not the people coming for them were the Americans of Team Reaper or the White Wolf's own forces.

Chandler and Crisfulli stepped to the back of the

galley, a narrower space, where the mercenary captain tried to raise Jackson on the mobile radio unit, which, because the signals bounced off a satellite, easily reached the villa.

No response. And because of the sat link, no static.

"If there's another boat coming," Chandler said, "we have to assume Jackson is dead, and Bascomb is free."

"I need you and Rosen up top and ready to fight," Crisfulli said.

"We came prepared," the mercenary said. He brushed past Crisfulli to collect Rosen, and they opened a small closet in the galley and began removing weapons from inside.

Don Mateo kept the throttle open as he steered the Malibu over the choppy waters, the boat bouncing, sea spray assaulting John Kane and Borden Hunt as they crouched behind the cockpit.

Leland Bascomb stayed hunkered down at the stern, where the narrow space of a seat and a portion of the gunwale kept him out of sight. He was concealed, but not covered. A bullet could easily pass through the hull and into his body should one hit just right. They all faced the same risk, of course. Kane had told Bascomb to stay low but didn't tell him how quite unprotected he really was.

"How much farther?" Kane shouted to Mateo.

"Visual contact in two minutes," Mateo said, after consulting his instruments. The Malibu wasn't as fancy as the Evo 43, but it too contained a small radar unit that Mateo referred to.

Kane knew without being told, though, that if they could see the Crisfulli vessel on radar, the reverse was true.

Which means they were speeding into a fight with no

element of surprise. This would be a head-on attack. No holds barred. Chief Hunt had prepared for such an occasion, and the surprise item in the "big case of whoop ass" had greatly pleased John "Reaper" Kane.

The toy was the big gun, a Maxwell Atchisson AA-12 full-auto shotgun, capable of delivering a sustained blast of Double-O buck at the hull of the Crisfulli vessel. Unless the boat was armor-plated, no craft could sustain the level of damage delivered by the AA-12. It was good for taking down men, too. Borden Hunt liked versatility. Hunt slung the HK 416 across his back and removed the big AA-12 from the case, a drum magazine already in place, and loaded with 32 Double-O buck shells. The tall sights, front and rear, provided for excellent target acquisition, and the gas-operated recoil system made recoil almost non-existent. Muzzle flip would not be a problem once Hunt unleashed a stream of buckshot.

Mateo did a double-take as Hunt readied the AA-12. "Hubba hubba," he said.

"I don't like their chances," Hunt said.

Kane only grinned as he tucked the HK 416 into his shoulder. "We got a boat!" he shouted.

The dark outline of the Evo 43, visible in the glow of the moon, was still too far away to shoot, but the object grew as the Malibu continued its approach. Mateo cut back the throttle a little, but the boat continued forward, the motor in the center of the boat's underbelly chugging along with little strain.

Something flashed against the dark outline of the enemy boat, the orange trail of a rocket homing in on the Malibu.

"Here comes the red carpet!" Chief Hunt yelled, as he ran to the forward seating area at the bow and dropped low, propping the fully-automatic shotgun on the gunwale. Still too far away for an effective shot.

Mateo pushed the throttle forward, the Malibu's speed picking up. As the rocket neared, he turned swiftly to starboard, steering the boat in a wide arc. Seconds later the rocket smacked into the water where the Malibu had been, the shockwave of the resulting explosive blast kicking up a spray of water that landed nowhere near Kane and his crew. Mateo completed the wide turn, straightening the wheel to aim the Malibu at the enemy boat once again.

"If they keep shooting rockets, we'll never get close enough!" Hunt shouted over the spray of water and the noise of the engine.

"Make it hard for them, Don," Kane said.

Mateo steered a zig-zag pattern, trying to vary the zigs and zags to keep the enemy from predicting their direction. A second rocket flashed. The second projectile lifted slightly as it traveled, passing overhead, the heat of the back blast washing over Kane's neck.

"Hard to aim when the water's choppy," Mateo said.

"We can't count on that happening again. That first rocket was dead on," Kane said. His hands were wet. He wiped them on his fatigue pants, which were also wet, thus doing no good. He gripped his weapon again and hoped his hands didn't slip during firing.

Because now they were within firing range.

The AA-12 announced their arrival, Chief Hunt squeezing off a three-round burst, the *boom boom boom* loud even over the noise of the environment, bodies on the enemy boat ducking for cover as the steel balls of buckshot smacked into the hull of the boat.

Mateo turned away to avoid a collision, Kane adding to the gunfire with a controlled burst from the Heckler & Koch

416. The rough water made precision shooting tough. None of his rounds connected, but he did see somebody on the boat lift his own rifle to fire back. Kane saw the flaming muzzle of the man's weapon, almost a strobe effect against the enemy boat's black background, but the rounds came nowhere near the Malibu.

Mateo executed another turn.

"They must have used up the rockets!" Mateo told Kane.

"We should have brought some of our own," Kane said.

"They wouldn't fit in the big case of whoop ass!" Hunt shouted back.

As the Malibu continued its turn, Kane snapped a look back at Leland Bascomb. The ocean explorer was flat on the deck, both hands covering his neck, and soaked. He glanced up at Kane, too, and smiled, flashing Reaper One a brief thumbs up.

Mateo straightened the boat once again.

"Get down!" Hunt shouted.

The big Evo 43 raced by at full power, the roar of the motors canceling out any other sound. Two men fired on the Malibu, the bullets smacking into the fiberglass frame, Kane returning fire, Hunt racing headlong to the stern with the AA-12 bucking against his shoulder. He fired once burst, then another, at the retreating yacht. He lowered the weapon with a curse.

Kane checked himself first. No holes he hadn't been born with. He looked at Mateo, who appeared uninjured, and was twisting the wheel to pursue the other boat. Leland Bascomb also appeared uninjured but stuck his head up long enough to see what was happening.

"We can't catch them, John!" Mateo said. The throttle

lever was all the way forward. "I'm giving her everything she's got."

Kane told him to do his best. They hadn't counted on a pursuit. Kane, now that he considered their rush to engage the enemy hadn't taken much into account other than their supposed superior firepower. It was a cinch now that Ceasario Crisfulli had the Sanchez money, and would reach shore before they did. It was an even further cinch that either Crisfulli would leave somebody behind to try and take out Kane, Hunt, and Don and his wife, or they'd simply get on a plane with the money and move on to their next destination. Kane had no idea what Crisfulli's agenda truly was, so he couldn't decide which option he'd take.

But as the Malibu continued after the ever-vanishing Evo 43, Kane looked around. At least Mateo and Leland Bascomb were still alive. No casualties would be added to the ever-growing list of individuals caught up in a war not their own.

Tonight, anyway.

Carlos Lorenzo kept an eye on the coolant temperature of the Evo 43's power plant. It remained in the green zone, but every now and then the needle pushed into the red.

But they had to escape the smaller boat. No question.

Crisfulli grabbed his arm. "Are you hurt?"

"No!"

Crisfulli checked Chandler, who reported the same. Rosen had been hit. Blood leaked from a tear on his right arm.

"One of those guys nicked me," he explained. "It's not bad."

"Stings from the salt?"

"Oh, it stings, all right."

Crisfulli and Rosen went below to treat and dress the wound. Bella Lane helped. When it was obvious, she knew more about such work than he, Crisfulli stepped back. He pounded a fist against a wall. He had hoped the Americans would only watch and observe and try to figure out what he was doing. A direct strike meant that they either knew, or suspected, what was actually going on. And, worse, Crisfulli did not have time to deal with them. They needed to get the money aboard their plane and get out of the Bahamas. The Americans might lose track of him. There was no way they'd be able to follow him to the lair of the White Wolf.

He hoped.

His own direct strike against Team Reaper might prove useful, but it meant diverting Chandler and other resources to Texas, to attack the team's headquarters, but that might not hurt the members of the field team, and Crisfulli needed Chandler to organize the rest of his mercenary squads for the attack on the Wolf.

Crisfulli had no choice but to carry on and shake the pursuit.

He was so close to victory that he wasn't going to let Team Reaper ruin his plans.

They found Katie Mateo pacing in the hotel room she shared with her husband.

As she and Don embraced, Kane told Bascomb to get in the shower and clean up. They weren't staying long.

"You're all a mess," Katie said, her eyes moving up and down at Kane and Hunt.

Kane laughed. He wanted to say, "You should see the

other guy," but there was no point. The *other guy* might have escaped without a scratch.

"You two need to get out of here, ASAP," Kane said.

"No flights till morning," Don Mateo said.

"You're leaving with us. Private jet, courtesy of Uncle Sam. Get packed."

"What?" Katie asked.

Kane stepped close to the woman. "We lost them, Katie. They have what they came for, and they aren't sticking around. They may leave somebody here to try and kill us, and I can't have that. Especially not you two."

Katie Mateo took a deep breath. "I suppose you can't."

"I've buried enough friends as it is," Kane said, with a glance at Don.

Don nodded.

"Hurry and pack," Kane said. "I'll go back to my room and do the same."

"Where's all your gear?" Katie asked.

Hunt said, "Trade secret, ma'am. But weapons are secured."

"You'll want that, too, right?" She pointed at the Russian machine pistol on the nightstand.

Hunt snatched the weapon, ejecting the magazine and clearing the firing chamber. "Yup. You know how expensive these things are?"

General Mary Thurston wasn't happy.

"Our transport jets aren't meant for civilians, Reaper."

"I'm making an exception in this case, ma'am. We have two American citizens that need to get out of the field of fire, and somebody needs to take care of Leland Bascomb.

We can pick up the Crisfulli trail after we drop them off. What's happening in Montenegro?"

"We're not done, Reaper."

"We can argue later, ma'am. What's the other team's status?"

Thurston said nothing. Kane waited her out. If the general wanted to argue about his field decisions at this time, he'd quit without a second thought. There was only so much of her he could take, sometimes.

But Thurston put away the hatchet for the time being and updated Kane on the goings-on overseas.

"Did we get anything out of the effort?" Kane asked.

"A whole bunch of phone numbers, voice mails, virtually who's-who of the French-Italian Corridor," Thurston said. "It does not appear that Cote and Crisfulli have been working together, however. We think Cote was killed to keep us from getting to her.

"Cara is working with Slick on the digital information," she continued, "and we put in a request to MI5 to question the two thugs Crisfulli left in London to guard Bascomb's family. Maybe they'll have something we can use."

"Crisfulli holds all the cards right now, ma'am."

"We're aware, Reaper. But don't worry. We're going to reshuffle the deck."

CHAPTER 14

Back aboard his private jet, Ceasario Crisfulli sat near the case of money. It was jammed under the table in front of his chair, in plain view. He hadn't counted the cash yet, and had, so far, resisted all attempts to fondle the money. He wasn't going to have it for very long, and there was no reason to form an attachment to the American greenbacks. He knew the case was supposed to contain six million dollars, and he doubted Jorge Sanchez had miscounted.

His crew had made it aboard the jet and out of the Bahamas alive, albeit the late departure stunned the normally sleepy nighttime crew at the airport tower. Didn't matter. They were airborne and heading back to France. The next phase of his plan would be underway within 24 hours; his goal within reach, he allowed himself a sense of satisfaction. *Almost there.*

All was well until Bella Lane sat down in the chair to his right. The look on her face alarmed him, but he showed no reaction.

He raised a curious eyebrow instead. "Yes?"

"Desire Cote is dead."

"The Americans?"

"No. A sniper got her."

Crisfulli nodded. "The Wolf is cleaning house."

It made sense. The old man didn't know who to trust after the affair with Aymard Caron, and he'd decided to wipe out the upper echelon, leaving only Crisfulli on the playing field. It was easier to deal with one enemy than several, and with both Caron and Cote gone, Crisfulli would have an easier job of taking over. On the opposite side of the coin, the White Wolf would only face one adversary. He laughed. Either the Americans or the Wolf were doing half his work for him.

Crisfulli made eye contact with Chandler, who sat on the other side of the cabin.

Neither said anything. The mercenary captain had spent the last hour on the phone himself, waking up other members of his team all over the world, telling them to make tracks for a specific rendezvous point in France.

Crisfulli's army was about to assemble.

He said to Bella Lane, "There's nothing we can do except keep moving forward. By this time tomorrow, it won't matter what the Wolf, or Adalene Severin, does. They can't stop us."

Bella Lane nodded and returned to her computer.

Team Reaper Headquarters
El Paso, TX

"What do you have, Slick?"

Sam "Slick" Swift, the red-headed hacker of Team Reaper's Bravo Team, was getting tired of the question. Every ten minutes, it seemed, General Thurston was visiting his workstation to ask the same question.

He didn't totally blame her, but she was becoming a baby diaper. Full of shit and always on his ass.

At least this time, unlike her previous visits, he had news.

"Communication is spiking on all the numbers we have off Desire Cote's phone," he said.

General Thurston leaned over his shoulder to look at Slick's computer screen. The columns of numbers and associated boxes showing active sound waves meant nothing to her.

"Explain."

"News of her murder is spreading, and they're all talking about it."

"Anything we can use?"

"There's a couple of guys who think Crisfulli is behind the killing, and that it ties in with him wanting to knock over the White Wolf, but—"

"That's nothing we don't suspect already."

"At least we're not the only things thinking about the idea. Now we know for sure."

"I need something we can *act* on, Slick. Right *now*."

"All I can do is sort the data, ma'am."

"Sort faster," she ordered.

"Where's Kane?" Swift asked.

"On his way back, and then if I don't fire him, he'll be on his way to Montenegro. Keep at it."

"There's one more thing, ma'am."

"What?"

"Since Reaper One told us about the mercenary named Chandler, I've been keeping tabs on other freelancers Chandler has been associated with. He hires often and pulls from the usual crew of mercs running around Europe."

"And?"

"Quite a few are suddenly no longer at home."

"Where are they going?"

"Not sure. Yet."

"Tell me when you are sure."

Thurston pivoted on a heel and walked away, leaving Swift wondering why she'd even suggest getting rid of Reaper One. It was quite unlike her to speak that way.

Swift cleared the sound waves from his screen and returned to the list of cell phone numbers, watching the software record each call. Somewhere in those conversations was the next lead they required, and Swift wouldn't stop until he found what the team needed.

Haguenau, France

Ceasario Crisfulli had heard all his life, when it comes to money, "Don't spend it all in one place."

But he quite enjoyed dropping six million dollars as soon as he had the money in his possession.

The tranquility of the Forest of Haguenau was this day disturbed by over 60 men, heavily armed, preparing to advance on a target. Most were foot soldiers. They'd be pointed at the target and told to attack. Chandler and Rosen would act as an advance party, and rig explosives on the White Wolf's known escape routes to keep him trapped on his property. Crisfulli wasn't going to let his quarry escape through his usual sleight-of-hand tricks.

The forest was well east of Paris, close to the German border, and the largest undivided forest in all of France. It was possible for one to disappear in this forest. Very possible.

Crisfulli would have liked a clear area for the meeting point, but instead had to contend with uneven terrain and a plethora of trees and foliage. The mercenaries didn't seem to mind. Most of them appeared to know each other and talked like old friends as they prepared.

All Crisfulli could do was pace, observe, and think.

The one fly in the ointment was Adalene Severin. Was she back at the Wolf's Lair where he could dispose of her, or was she somewhere else? If she remained on the loose, she would be a problem for sure. Like the White Wolf, she knew how to hide. Crisfulli might never have his chance to break her slender neck.

Normally such a loose end wouldn't bother Crisfulli. But she'd want revenge on *him* after what he had planned for the White Wolf, which meant he'd have to live behind more armor than existed in the world to avoid her wrath.

Somehow, he'd prevail. He noted, as he watched the mercenaries prepare, and examined some of their heavy transport, that everything had swung his way so far. A little more patience and he'd have Adalene Severin at the end of a rope.

Adalene Severin was back in the lair. She arrived via helicopter, and as the pilot made a swooping turn over the mountain top property where the White Wolf made his home, she once again marveled at what could only be called a palace.

The double rooftops poked through the canopy of trees which otherwise shielded the building, at least from above. On the ground, if one could climb that high, the open court-yard in front and the multi-level turret-roof design, complete with a one-lane access road, would be easy to see. It was the courtyard that the pilot aimed for, where the Wolf had placed a proper landing pad. The courtyard ended at a grass field, which then stretched to a drop off where the trees took over. The open field circled the property, the surrounding trees creating a natural enclosure. It was treacherous terrain to navigate, as the palace sat atop a mountain, but a dedi-cated crew could make the journey. The access road was the easiest entry point, one that Adalene often felt needed more security. But the White Wolf didn't agree. He felt his secu-rity arrangements were good enough, especially the steps taken to assure his anonymity and mystery. You can't find a man who doesn't exist.

The pilot lowered the chopper carefully. He didn't want a sudden gust of wind to push him into the trees or into the building itself.

Jean-Bernard Page, the White Wolf, waited a few yards away from the landing pad, a hat on his head to shield his face from the sun. The landing pad had no tree cover, and the overhead sun was bright.

The chopper touched down, and the pilot began to power down the machine. Adalene Severin did not wait. She exited the chopper, Voltaire the mercenary following, and she trotted toward the Wolf while Voltaire walked steadily. By the time they reached the old man, the rotor blades had gone silent, and the wind was rustling the trees.

"Welcome home," said the Wolf.

"Mission accomplished."

"Good. You're needed here. Ceasario is close."

"How can you tell?"

"It's a feeling. He is coming home."

The White Wolf turned and headed for a recessed doorway, in front of which stood an armed guard complete with camo uniform and automatic rifle. The guard opened the door and stepped aside. The Wolf entered first. Adalene and Voltaire followed. As she stepped through the threshold, Adalene marveled at the size of the building. She felt like an ant in comparison.

"If he's close," Adalene said as they walked along a dark-paneled ornate hallway, "why are we waiting? Attack while he's preparing."

"That won't be necessary, my dear. We will deal with him when he arrives."

"Do we have enough men?"

"My usual complement of troops is present."

"That's only six men!"

"There's also you and Mr. Voltaire."

Adalene, for the first time in a long time, felt nervous.

"I don't understand any of this!" she shouted.

The Wolf stopped. They had reached a winding staircase with gold rails, and a long red carpet draped over the steps.

"My dear," he said, "look at me."

She examined his face. His old face. The wrinkles, the large nose, the thick neck. He wore his usual white shirt and black jacket, and his belly bulged beneath both.

"How much longer do you think I have to live?" he asked.

Adalene blinked.

"Despite the ideas of some," the Wolf said, "I am not a God. We must all face our end. Perhaps my end will come at the hands of Ceasario."

"Then why did you have me—"

He held up a hand. She stopped talking.

"This is a conflict only me and Ceasario can finish," he said. "I did not want anybody else involved. Desire Cote is easily replaced; so is Aymard Caron. You see, my dear, Ceasario believes *me* to be responsible for the death of somebody he loved. If he's willing to kill me over that misunderstanding, it is foolish to think I can stop him. I am an old man, and one way or another, I will be departing this world sooner rather than later."

"Did you kill this person?"

The White Wolf took a few minutes to explain the situation between him, Ceasario, and the younger man's late girlfriend, Ariana. He ended with, "I did not kill Ariana. Why would I? And then keep Ceasario in the organization? For what, to mock him? Laugh behind his back? That makes no sense. Had I done what he accuses me of, I would have killed them both. Ariana died in an auto crash. There is nothing more sinister at work in this case than bad luck and human tragedy. But poor Ceasario believes otherwise. He's tortured himself into planning a scheme to kill me and take over because of this."

"You knew from the moment I brought Caron to you what was happening, didn't you?"

"Yes."

"And you think you can talk Ceasario out of killing you?"

The old man shrugged. "Who knows?"

Adalene only stared at the man. She felt Voltaire beside her, but the mercenary didn't speak.

Jean-Bernard Page turned and slowly climbed the steps. "I suggest you come with me, my dear. You also, Mr. Voltaire. We have guests to prepare for."

The lack of sentries bothered Chandler.

He and Rosen, dressed for battle, hid in bushes a stone's throw away from a cave opening. The mouth of the cave was dark, as he expected, but if this was the exit of an escape tunnel under the White Wolf's palace, surely there'd be troopers present.

He and Rosen remained firmly planted in their position, listening, eyes scanning for danger. None presented itself.

"Is the cave trapped?" Rosen asked.

"How?"

"Explosives, perhaps? Bombs that need to be deactivated before anyone can exit?"

"Via a panel inside the cave?"

"It's possible. Crisfulli says it's wired for light."

"We aren't going to find out by staying here. Come on."

With his automatic rifle tucked into his shoulder, ready for anything, Chandler left the bush and approached the cave. Rosen followed a few steps behind. They ascended the incline, the stone mouth growing as they neared. Chandler dropped to a knee, close enough to touch the cave. He ran his eyes up, around, and down the mouth. No explosive trap presented itself.

"We're clear," he said.

Rosen set down his rifle and removed the backpack he wore. Quickly opening the zipper, he handed Chandler a brick of plastic explosive and removed another for himself. They stepped toward the cave. Placing both bricks at either side of the entry, they then connected both via wire. Chandler's last act was to push an antenna into his brick, one that would receive the remote signal to detonate prior to the beginning of the attack.

Chandler and Rosen picked up their rifles and retraced their path back to the route they'd taken from the staging area. The bombs were set. Now all they needed was for the final stage of Crisfulli's plan to begin.

Jean-Bernard Page entered his den.

More dark paneling, full bookcases of books that actually looked read judging by the cracked spines, Renaissance artwork adorning the walls. Adalene had seen it before. Voltaire, not at all. He whistled at the sight, moving quickly to one of the Rembrandt's to admire the art on the canvas.

"This looks original," the mercenary said.

"It is," said the Wolf, as he pulled up on his trousers and eased into the chair behind a huge oak desk.

Adalene remained standing.

"Sit down, my dear."

Adalene complied, dropping onto a couch against the wall to the left of the old man's desk. Next to the couch stood a large wooden cabinet. Voltaire continued roaming the right-side wall, taking in the artwork.

"You're a connoisseur, Mr. Voltaire?"

"Oh, yes," said the mercenary. "I've tried my hand at painting." He didn't look at the Wolf, engrossed in the paintings. "I'm nowhere near as good as the masters, however."

"Nobody is. That's why they're the masters."

Voltaire laughed. After examining the last painting in the row, he joined Adalene on the other end of the couch.

Jean-Bernard Page rocked back in his chair.

"Are we going to simply sit here and wait?" Adalene asked.

Jean-Bernard Page closed his eyes. "Patience, Adalene. And, yes, the cabinet to your right contains a set of fully automatic rifles, should you need them."

CHAPTER 15

The last of the mercenaries arrived at the staging area.

At the same time, Chandler and Rosen returned with their report that the escape tunnel could be sealed with the flick of a switch once the fighting started.

Ceasario Crisfulli took the news with a slow nod.

He stood in front of a transport vehicle, the tires of which were almost the length of his legs. Bella Lane occupied the passenger seat in the cabin.

"I'll be with you shortly," Crisfulli announced. "Do a final inspection, and we'll start."

Crisfulli, as he climbed behind the wheel of the transport, felt like he sounded as if they were preparing to watch a football match.

But he wasn't detached from his goal. The end remained a fixed point in his mind.

He pulled the cabin door shut.

Bella Lane sat with a laptop, the screen aglow, albeit muted from the sunlight.

"We'll start soon," he said in a low voice.

"I heard."

"I want you to make your way into the town before we move out. Go to the safehouse. I have a project for you."

He explained.

She said okay.

"If you don't hear from me within a few hours, send a note to the Americans like last time."

"What should I tell them?"

"Where to find the bodies. Because if Jean-Bernard Page or Adalene Severin succeed in killing me, I'll leave it to them to finish what I started."

Bella Lane stared at him with soft eyes.

"Do not be afraid, darling. It's simply an insurance policy."

"I don't like it."

"It's necessary." Crisfulli opened the driver's door. "You should leave. Now."

Crisfulli dropped to the ground as Bella Lane closed her laptop.

The springs on Jean-Bernard Page's chair squeaked as he lightly rocked back and forth. His eyes were fixed on the ceiling.

Adalene sat on the couch, rage growing inside her. In any normal situation, if she tried to leave, the old man would order her death. She wouldn't make one step out the door. Now? She thought she could walk right out, and the old man would keep rocking in his chair.

But there was no way she was going to leave. Jean-Bernard Page had given her the second, and maybe the third, chance at a full life. She'd have been dead long ago had it not been for his guiding hand. No. She'd stay to the end and kill Crisfulli herself if it came to that. And she hoped that's exactly what happened.

"They're coming," Jean-Bernard Page said.

Adalene sat up sharply. She heard the sound too. Helicopters. Multiple helicopters. An alarm blared somewhere on the property, but the old man didn't leave his chair. He closed his eyes once again.

Adalene left the couch, opening the cabinet, and selected a rifle. She tossed it to Voltaire. She picked another for herself, grabbing already loaded magazines for both weapons. She gave a few to Voltaire and jammed the remaining in the pockets of her jeans, slapping one of them into the action. She yanked back the charging handle to chamber the first round. She did not bother flicking the safety catch.

Four helicopters began to circle the Wolf's palace, the side doors of each opening. As the choppers positioned themselves over the courtyard, ropes dropped from each helicopter, men in fatigues and carrying their tools of destruction sliding down the ropes.

The Crisfulli troops went into action straight away, firing on the Wolf soldiers who ventured outside, the crackling barrage of automatic weapons fire barely rising above the volume of the helicopter engines.

As the Wolf troopers fell, the first of four transports drove onto the courtyard, having made the journey up the one-lane access road without resistance. More mercenaries jumped out of the back of each, swarming the property, their weapons probing for threats of any kind. They found none. By the time Crisfulli himself arrived, exiting the transport with Chandler and Rosen beside him, the mercenaries had set up a perimeter around the courtyard, waiting for the fight to continue.

While Chandler and Rosen toted automatic rifles, Crisfulli's armament consisted only of a Model 92FS 9mm Beretta pistol, which he held in his right hand.

He nodded once to Chandler, who used his left hand to grab for the remote detonator in a pocket of his combat vest. As if turning on a light switch, he pressed the button on the remote. A dull thud rocked the mountain.

Crisfulli smiled.

"Into the lair, my friends," he announced, boldly crossing the courtyard to the entryway, stepping around the dead bodies of the Wolf's soldiers. Chandler shouted orders to his men. The choppers pulled away. Soon only the wind and rustling trees made any noise whatsoever.

Crisfulli entered the palace. Down the ornate hallway, to the spiral staircase. He walked with confidence while Chandler and Rosen swept the area, the muzzles of their weapons moving with their eyes.

Crisfulli started up the staircase. His shoes made a light noise on the carpeted steps.

To the second floor.

Down a wide hallway.

The double-doors of the den were wide open.

Movement!

Crisfulli saw the two gunners first; each one positioned on either side of the doorway. One of them had long blonde hair. A woman. *Adalene! Yes!*

The other Crisfulli didn't recognize. He raised the Beretta and fired twice, moving to the right wall as Chandler and Rosen opened fire. The fusillade of lead chopped through the wall and doorframe, splinters and sheetrock dust flying. The man cried out sharply once and fell to the floor. The woman returned fire, screaming before another burst from Chandler's gun created a sprout of red roses across her chest. She jerked with the hits, collapsing, moving no more.

Crisfulli hurried to the doorway, his right arm extended with the snout of the Beretta 92FS leading the way.

He stepped over the bodies and stopped.

"Ceasario," the White Wolf said. "Welcome home."

Crisfulli needed only a second to assess the situation.

"You've been waiting for me?"

"I knew this day would come."

Crisfulli eyed the old man behind the big desk. With the bright sun coming through the window to the man's back, his features were hard to discern. But there was no mistaking who sat in the chair. The chair Crisfulli intended to occupy.

"Then you know why I'm going to kill you."

"Over a mistake, Ceasario. A mistake."

"You murdered Ariana on purpose. You murdered her because she chose *me*. What were you thinking?"

"I did not have her murdered, Ceasario. You've had the wrong idea in your head for too long. What did I have to gain by killing her?"

"Make me suffer."

"Why would I do that?"

"Because you're cruel."

"No crueler than you, Ceasario. We are two of the same kind."

Crisfulli's grip tightened on the Beretta. The hammer

was back, the trigger reset and primed for another squeeze. Yet he didn't squeeze. He wanted to hear the old man beg for his life before killing him.

Cruel, yeah.

That was the way of the world.

"Ariana's death was a tragedy, Ceasario. The greater tragedy is you driving yourself into a rage because you believed I was responsible. It made no sense to kill Ariana and let you live, for the very reason you think I did kill her. For the very reason we're talking right now. Do you think I'd let you live knowing you'd someday be pointing a gun at my head?"

Crisfulli's aim remained steady. He was waiting. Waiting for the begging to begin.

"Put down the gun."

"No."

"We need to discuss our future like normal adults, Ceasario. I forgive you for all this killing on my property. I forgive you for killing poor Adalene. Put down your weapon, and we'll talk about the future. You and I, together, can continue to operate our business, side-by-side, as if we were father and son. When my time comes, you will take over. A proper transition. My gift to you."

"Never."

"Then kill me. Shoot me and take this chair. Take over the whole Corridor. You'll have what you want. What you think you want. What you won't have is peace, because you'll live the rest of your life wondering if you truly made the right decision, or if I'm telling you the truth."

Crisfulli blinked.

"I could have met you with as great a force as you've dropped on my doorstep, Ceasario. The force you spent so much time and effort to acquire the money for because you thought using your own funds would tip me off. But I didn't. I wanted to see you up close. I wanted to talk."

"And beg for your life?"

Jean-Bernard Page laughed a hearty laugh.

"Is that what you're waiting for? No, Ceasario, there will be no begging. I will stand up and let you shoot me if that's what your heart desires. As I said to poor Adalene before your men filled her with holes, I'm old. I'm not going to last much longer. If there's going to be a change in leadership, you should be the one who takes control. You were always the best of us."

The Beretta spoke once. The flash from the muzzle blocked Crisfulli's view of the old man for a moment, but when he lowered the gun, the old man was still in his chair. Slumped, almost slipping off the seat. A neat hole in his head trickled a line of blood onto his starched white shirt and the black tie.

Ceasario Crisfulli lowered the pistol. He blinked several times as his eyes lingered on the dead man before him.

He jammed the gun in the waistband of his pants and approached the desk quickly. Behind him, he heard Chandler speaking into a radio, advising the mercenaries outside to search the property for any remaining Wolf troopers and to shoot them on sight.

Crisfulli touched the warm dead body. The old man's eyes remained open. He grabbed the old man by the hair and lifted the face to see directly into those dead eyes. Looking for something. The truth, maybe? The hand holding the hair began to shake. Crisfulli ignored the shaking. But he couldn't ignore what was going through his mind and body.

Instead of satisfaction, he felt doubt.

A great deal of doubt.

CHAPTER 16

Montenegro
   Oasis Resort

Cara Billings answered the knock on the door and smiled when she saw John Kane standing before her.

"About time you caught up," she said. She let him in. He pushed the door shut.

The "Lucky" Casino was too hot for Cara and the rest of Team Reaper to remain. After the police were done with their investigation, which lasted well into the morning hours of the next day following Desire Cote's murder, she, Brick, Axe, Traynor, and Arenas had relocated to the Oasis to wait for further orders. They didn't bother checking out the amenities the resort offered. They weren't going to be there long enough to enjoy the perks; at least, they hoped they weren't going to be there long.

Cara knew from an update with General Mary Thurston that Kane had returned to the United States with his two friends, the Mateos, and Leland Bascomb, the British oceanographer. The Brit was home now, put on a plane before being in the US for an hour, and returned home to reunite with his family. The Mateos also departed for home and the official end to a very eventful vacation.

Thurston ended the update advising Cara that Kane was on his way, but without Hunt. The Navy SEAL had other duties to attend to now that his assignment to provide aid to Kane had finished.

But they still had nothing to go on. Sam "Slick" Swift was still sorting and monitoring for information from Desire Cote's phone.

"How was Nassau?" Cara asked.

Kane gave her a complete update as they sat around the room's table. At the end, she said, "I have a feeling—"

"What?"

"You didn't try as hard because you were trying to protect your friends."

Kane stared at her a moment. "We've lost enough people," he said.

"Luna Blaise?"

"She's on my mind, yeah. Her and her people."

"Did you do all you could do in Nassau, Reaper?"

Kane looked at the carpet. "I don't know. I kept my friends alive."

"But Crisfulli escaped."

"We'll get him."

"How many more people will he kill before we do?"

He looked at her sharply. "Hopefully only those that deserve it."

"Who will get caught in the crossfire?"

"Are you trying to be my conscience or something, Cara?"

"I'm trying to keep you from making mistakes that will cause the very destruction you're trying to prevent."

"You're saying I should have sacrificed my friends, and Bascomb, for a drug thug? That's not a noble exchange, Cara."

"You need a rest."

"Probably a long one," he said.

"When we're done, you should take it up with General Thurston."

"She and I have a lot to talk about already."

"What do you mean?"

Kane finally allowed himself a half-grin. "I've been naughty."

"Dammit, Reaper—"

"Too many victims, Cara. Far too many. I wasn't going to add my friends to the list. This isn't their fight."

"But it's *our* fight. That's why we do what we do."

"It's not enough," he said.

"What if we do nothing instead? People will keep dying. At least with us, we can save some."

"Some," he said.

"That's the way it is, Reaper."

"I'm supposed to accept that we have our fingers in the dike, but the boat is still sinking?"

"You're supposed to accept that we aren't the only ones fighting this way. You're putting too much on your own shoulders, Reaper."

He let out a sigh. Maybe she was right. He told her so.

"Was that hard to admit?"

"No."

"What do you want to do then?"

"I want to finish this fight. I want to put Crisfulli down like a sick dog, and then I want a vacation."

"You'll get that. And when you come back, we'll start again."

"An endless cycle," he said. "You're telling me it doesn't seem useless to you?"

"Maybe it does," she said, "but I have hope."

"Hope?"

"That maybe the next one will be the last. Or the one after that."

Kane had no reply. Maybe keeping Don Mateo and Leland Bascomb on the boat, while they chased after Crisfulli, had been a mistake. But he hadn't wanted to lose any time, so it made sense to keep them along. He and Hunt could have easily driven the Malibu boat, and maybe, without the chance of collateral damage, been more aggressive. Maybe they could have stopped Crisfulli cold instead of letting him get away. But, then again, the Malibu hadn't been able to keep up with the faster craft.

"It beats dwelling on the alternative," she added.

Kane remained silent. He wanted his phone to ring. He wanted to hear Thurston's voice with the next lead.

The lead they needed to finish the job.

And then his phone did ring.

Thurston and Swift, over the speakerphone, waited while Cara called the rest of the team, and they huddled close to the phone while the general and red-headed hacker spoke.

"Crisfulli has finally screwed up," the general said.

"How?" Kane asked.

"He insists on using email to communicate with the Corridor distributors," she said, adding: "Slick?"

Sam Swift took over the conversation.

"Yesterday we got a spike of activity on the phone

numbers we pulled from Desire Cote's cell phone," the hacker said. "Not phone calls, but emails, and almost everybody on the list checked their email using the phone.

"Crisfulli has apparently taken down the White Wolf and is now in overall charge of the French-Italian Corridor. The emails are from his associate, a woman named Bella Lane, whom we assume sent the original email regarding Axe's whereabouts.

"The emails explain the transition of leadership, and that all Corridor functions are to continue as normal, and that Crisfulli himself will be coming out to speak to everybody one-by-one, as time permits."

"Great," Cara said. "We intercept him when he hits the road."

"This is where they screwed up, Cara," Swift said. "We were able to trace the email this time."

Kane perked up. "Where?"

"A town in France called Haguenau. Maybe 'town' is generous. It's more of a village. Very small. Very much in the boonies. And they notice when things out of the ordinary happen."

"Like what?" Kane asked.

"Helicopters, explosions, men with guns, you know."

"Is that the town where the Wolf was hiding?"

"Near it, actually. He's in the adjoining forest, more isolated than the town if you can believe that. We did a satellite scan of the area and found the place. Crisfulli and his people are still in the process of stacking bodies, plus it was the only major structure in the area a chief drug thug might use as home base."

"Technology is great," Pete Traynor said, "until it isn't."

Kane asked, "What's the plan, General?"

Thurston replied, "This operation is ending where it

began, so we're going to finish it the same as we started. French OCRTIS have been alerted, and they are waiting for you in Paris."

Kane blinked but said nothing.

"Who's going to meet us?" Cara asked.

"The new chief, you'll meet him when you get there. They are assembling a tactical team and will make room for you on the helicopters. We all have a stake in this one."

"No kidding," Kane said.

"Anything else?" Cara asked.

"Get your butts to Paris," the general said. "Now."

"Yes, ma'am," Cara said. She ended the call. "You heard the lady. I'll call the plane."

"Be ready to leave," Kane said, "in fifteen minutes."

The team assured him they didn't need that long.

Orly Airport, Paris
Eight Hours Later

John Kane stepped off the Team Reaper jet and onto the hot tarmac, where a lone man in front of an SUV greeted him. Behind the man were more SUVs, with, presumably, more OCRTIS operatives.

"Welcome back to Paris," the man said, his English good but accent thick. "My name is Xavier Rigal."

John Kane shook the man's hand. He was about as tall as Kane but looked older, his black hair grayer than the fellow probably cared to admit. Kane wanted to make a joke. "So, you're the next victim?" But he did not. The memory of Luna Blaise and her second-in-command Julian

Berenger was too strong in his mind to cut that low with somebody as equally affected by their deaths.

Luna especially.

"Thanks for having us. We know you're not obligated to have us here for the end."

"Least we can do," Rigal said. "We've already fought and shed blood together. We might as well finish it together. And if you're anything like me, you're wanting some payback."

"Oh, yes," Kane said. "Payback."

The remaining members of Team Reaper, along with Team Bravo operative Pete Traynor, descended from the jet. It took almost fifteen minutes to unload Reaper's gear from the jet's cargo hold, but soon people and gear were loaded onto the SUVs, and the convoy drove off the airport property.

Kane rode up front while Rigal drove. Kane's teammates took up space in the middle and back seats of the SUV.

"I'm close to retiring soon," Rigal said.

"Didn't want the job, I take it?"

"I wanted it," Rigal said, "especially after what happened to Blaise and Berenger. But it will be my last field assignment. I'm not going to take a desk job. I've been doing real work for too long. After this, and after we get OCRTIS straightened out after our unfortunate back-to-back tragedies, I'll spend the rest of my life fishing."

"That sounds like a great plan."

"My grandkids will enjoy it."

Kane grunted and fell silent. *It must be nice to have a family. Somebody to actually fight for, rather than fancy ideals that seem harder and harder to sacrifice for.* But then he checked his thoughts. If Cara Billings, despite her DNA strain of cynicism, considering all she'd already been through, could have hope that their mission against the cartels followed a path to victory, so could he.

And who knew? Maybe, at the end of that road, Kane might find something or someone worth settling down for.

"How are we fixed for a briefing?" Kane asked the Frenchman.

"First order of business. We're preparing a helicopter assault."

"Good." *No wasted time.*

Because there wasn't any time to waste. They didn't know how long Ceasario Crisfulli would stay at the White Wolf's palace, den, sanctuary, whatever they wanted to call the location. Unless he planned on spending a few days using the gold-plated bathroom or whatever other insane luxuries the Wolf had installed, paid for by the deaths and misery of his product's end-users. There could be no other reason Crisfulli wanted the chair than greed. Greed dominated the goals and desires of so many cartel thugs Kane had crossed. He was genuinely surprised when he found one not looking for all the money in the world.

Xavier Rigal drove on.

OCRTIS Headquarters
Paris

Rigal led the convoy through thick Paris street traffic to a tall obviously government building somewhere in the city. With all the various signs and busyness around him, Kane wasn't paying attention to where they were. And the Frenchman didn't give him time to acclimate. The convoy zoomed through the opening of the underground garage beneath the building. With orders to "Leave your gear," they took an elevator ride up to a top floor, where a group of people waited around a conference table.

The big oak wood table sat in the center of the brightly lighted room, one wall consisting of wide panes of glass and looking out over Paris. Cara whistled. Kane nudged her to a chair. Maybe they'd have time to appreciate the view once the briefing was over.

Rigal introduced the other OCRTIS officials and dimmed the lights. Sitting behind a laptop connected to a projector, he flashed on a wall screen details of their target.

Kane noted no refreshments on the table. OCRTIS wasn't kidding around. Business only.

Their blood was boiling, and they wanted a fight.

Big time.

Kane didn't blame them.

Rigal said, "What we are looking at is basically a castle from the outside. We have no idea what it looks like on the inside. Nobody has ever seen this property before."

The overhead shot showed a building with its roofs almost covered by a thick layer of treetops.

"If you zoom in, you can see the front courtyard with the landing pad, and this grassy field that stretches around the length of the property. There is one access road, right here."

Brick let out a curse.

"Something on your mind, Brick?" Kane asked.

"Man, that's a lot of open space for a fight."

"What's covered by those trees, Xavier?"

The Frenchman said, "Our best overheard pictures show a drop-off. Not very steep, it's not a cliff, but enough foliage by which we can get bogged down if we try a land assault. That's why we're using helicopters."

Back to the overhead shot.

"Our plan," Rigal said, "is to drop our forces in the front, and in the back, and get into the castle from either side."

"No way."

All eyes snapped to Axe Burton.

"What's on your mind, Axe?" Kane asked.

"Those open areas around the castle are death traps," Axe said. "The bad guys will have cover from inside the structure. That leaves us in the open to be picked off."

Rigal asked, "What is your suggestion?"

"Split into three groups. Two can take the front and back after the first team enters through the roof. A shaped charge can open a hole big enough for us to get through."

Xavier Rigal looked at the map, then back at Axe.

"I think you're right," the Frenchman said. "That will be our approach."

One of the OCRTIS officials, not speaking English, asked a question.

"The question is," Rigal said, to the annoyed look of the official, "what is our objective?" Rigal's eyes swept the officials and stopped at John Kane.

"Mr. Kane, care to answer that one?"

"Are you sure I answer for your people?"

"Luna trusted you. So do I."

"We're going in there to get even," Kane said. "The people who killed Luna Blaise and Julian Berenger may have already been taken out by Ceasario Crisfulli, but their deaths mean nothing if Crisfulli is able to take full control of the French-Italian Corridor. If we have any chance of shutting down the operation, that chance is *today*.

Tomorrow he'll be too strong to stop, and he'll disappear same as his predecessor, and we'll have to start over. That's unacceptable to us, gentleman."

"And we don't," Xavier Rigal said, "intend on taking any prisoners."

One of the other officials argued that statement. Rigal shut him down.

"The time for arrest has passed," he said. "The deaths of our people cannot go unavenged."

More of the officials didn't like that, and Rigal engaged in a brief exchange with them, ending with, "Gentlemen, I don't have to do this. You've asked me to do this because you have nobody else. Would either one of you like to take on this mission?"

The officials didn't answer. They looked at each other blankly.

"I didn't think so," Rigal said. To the Americans, he added: "We launch in one hour."

"Music to our ears," Kane said.

CHAPTER 17

Dead men are heavier than ten bags of dry cement.

Ceasario Crisfulli watched the mercenaries in front of him part like the waves of the Red Sea as he carried Jean-Bernard Page's heavy body across his back, the old man's blood leaking onto his white suit, his weight bearing down on Crisfulli's frame. But Crisfulli persisted. He crossed the courtyard, onto the grass, heading for the edge of the property and the drop off where the trees began. The light tapping of heels behind him signified that Bella Lane followed. He took some comfort in that. It was hard not to feel totally alone after putting a bullet in the old man's head. It had been a long time since Crisfulli personally killed a man, and he forgot the toll it took on him. Deep down, he knew such an act wasn't natural; the other part of him was glad he'd finally done what he'd promised the late Ariana so many years ago.

Crisfulli reached the edge of the grass. There was no barrier between the grass and the slope of land beyond, and the trees, packed so close together, formed a never-ending snake of trucks. He grunted and heaved and tossed the corpse of the White Wolf off his back. The old man's big body hit the ground, arms and legs flailing about as his body tumbled down the slope, crashing into tree trunks, smashing foliage. The corpse slipped through the space between two trees and continued to tumble out of sight.

Crisfulli laughed.

"You look horrible," Bella Lane advised, looking him up and down.

"It's not my blood, darling," he said. "I'm going to wear it like a badge of honor until we're through here."

Crisfulli stopped talking, his eyes far away as he tried to trace the resting place of his adversary.

"You're worried about what he told you," Bella Lane said. She wore her red hair tied back in a ponytail.

"No."

"I can see it on your face, Ceasario."

The man in the blood-stained suit shook his head. "No."

"Then what do you really think?"

Crisfulli didn't hesitate with his answer. "I think he lied. He always lied. This was always a game to him. Always."

"I suppose it doesn't matter now," she said.

"The only thing that matters now is that we finish here. We have plenty of information to collect, all the files on our people, the ledgers regarding who he's been paying off in the government, the drug agents we turned into spies. All of that. Once it's collected, we are leaving."

Bella Lane asked, "Didn't he keep it on a computer? I can hack into his systems—"

"You don't get it, darling. Page never used computers. It's all on paper. There are three safes we have to empty."

"How soon?"

"Well," Crisfulli said, "it's not getting done while we

stand here talking about it. Let's go back inside and continue."

The two Leonardo AW109SP GrandNew helicopters, each bearing the seal of OCRTIS, flew north out of Paris, heading east for a flight just over four hours.

John Kane and Cara Billings represented Team Reaper in the first chopper, joined by Xavier Rigal and three of his OCRTIS Assault & Tactical SquadAssault & Tactical Squad. With their gear, the cramped cabin pushed them close together. The sun was already beginning to set. Their raid would be a nighttime attack after all.

Kane, Cara, and Rigal and his team took the time to look over maps and recon photos of the Wolf's lair, committing details to memory and discussing their attack plan.

Kane knew that whatever plan they cooked up would go out the window as soon as they met the first members of the opposition, but to have an overall strategy in place prior would mean less confusion when the fight started.

After a while, Kane sat back and looked out the window. The French countryside below looked serene. His thoughts strayed to Luna Blaise. He wondered what parts of the country she had liked most.

"What's on your mind?" Cara asked via their headphone intercom.

Kane didn't want to broadcast to the entire cabin, so he only shook his head. She did not ask a second time. Instead, she took hold of his right hand and squeezed. He looked at her. She smiled.

Despite their differences, she knew him better than anybody, and probably knew without him telling her exactly what he was thinking.

Too many had fallen, yeah. They'd almost lost Axe early on. Kane had fought to keep Don and Katie Mateo, and Leland Bascomb, the British ocean explorer, alive so they wouldn't be added to the list of the dead. He felt good about that. He felt good about having his team back together. They were doing what they did best, and Kane wouldn't have it any other way.

But they knew they were facing a force of hardened mercenaries, purchased with the Sanchez money Crisfulli had found. The battle would be fierce.

He hoped, when it was over, they were still together, one unit, ready to handle anything, but especially the next mission.

They started taking fire on the final approach.

"Hang on!" Rigal shouted over the headset, the pilot taking evasive action. The castle lay ahead, but in the dark, they saw nothing of the building. The winking muzzle flashes, however, were plainly visible.

Kane felt the bullets striking the body of the chopper, ineffectual at the distance, but serious, nonetheless. The co-pilot triggered the two rotating miniguns on either side of the cabin, and the chopper shook with the recoil of the weapons. A stream of tracer fire rocketed away from the chopper, zeroing on random targets, the pilot sweeping left and right to cover a wide area. The incoming fire ceased.

The second chopper broke off, keeping a short distance away while the pilot positioned the first chopper over a flat section of the roof. The side doors open. Team Reaper and the OCRTIS strike team rappelled down, Kane's stomach lurching as he fell through space, his boots hitting hard on the concrete roof. Their HK rifles were equipped with lights mounted on the forward grip. The bright light shined the way as they dropped onto the roof, the chopper pulling away, Kane and Cara moving forward to spread out the circular shaped charge in a wide enough circle to allow room for everybody to step through.

Rigal and one of his shooters anchored ropes to air conditioning boxes nearby, but they only had two attachment points. Two ropes meant they'd have to enter in pairs.

The first complication.

"Stand back!" Kane shouted as he readied the detonator for the shaped charge. The teams moved as far back as they could, almost the edge of the roof. Already, down below, mercenary troops were shouting at each other as they readied defensive positions.

Kane hit the button.

The shaped charge exploded downward with such force that the building shook, or at least the part of the building where the entry team stood. With a loud crash, the explosive broke through the cement, forcing chunks of debris into the floor below, creating a dust cloud, and a hole. Kane and Cara, grabbing the ropes, went in first.

Kane passed through the dark, surrounded by dust. The debris, upon landing, continued to kick up a cloud. His feet landed on solid floor, and he let go of the rope and grabbed for his lead weapon.

The HK 416 was strapped to his back, but he carried the Atchisson AA-12 automatic shotgun with which to clear the room. He scanned left, right, the flashlight on the front grip barely piercing the cloud of dust surrounding him. He saw enough to know there was nobody in the room, but the light did shine on a bed, mirrored closet doors, bathroom in the far corner. He shined the light on the door ahead. Solid oak with a gold knob. Cara landed behind him and snapped her HK into the ready position. They separated to allow space for the others to slide into the room.

"Looks like we blew up the big guy's bedroom," Cara said.

Kane didn't acknowledge. He glanced up at the hole as Rigal descended, then the three shooters from the Assault & Tactical Squad. Everybody spread out. There was plenty of space to do so in the big bedroom.

"This is Reaper One, we are inside, repeat, inside," Kane said into his com unit.

"Copy, Reaper One," the pilot of the first chopper replied.

"Reaper Four copies," said Axe Burton, in the second chopper with his part of the ground force.

Outside, the crackle of small-arms fire was overpowered by the chattering roar of the choppers' miniguns. The building shook with the impacts of the high-velocity bullets.

"Ground units ready to deploy," the second chopper pilot said.

Kane and the others ignored the call as Cara approached the door, the dust and smoke still thick in the room. She opened the door and looked into a long hallway. Pushing the door all the way open, she lifted the HK to her shoulder and exited the room with her head moving left and right.

Kane and the rest followed. The hallway was large enough to contain several M1 Abrams tanks side-by-side, with a tiled floor and wood columns.

Library to the left. Kane broke off to slip inside, passing the muzzle of the AA-12 around the bookcases, the chairs. No hostiles. He rejoined the others. "Clear."

Cara held up a hand and dropped to one knee. Kane, Rigal, and the other three shooters paused.

Their ears were still ringing from the shaped charge blast, but Kane soon picked up on what had captured Cara's attention.

Heavy boots.

Pounding up a flight of stairs.

"Spread out!" Kane shouted.

And then the shooting started.

The second chopper's miniguns blazed against the west side wall of the castle, portions of the wall crumbling under the onslaught of the barrage. Bodies of mercenaries already littered the concrete, but the grassy area prior to the trees looked clear.

Axe and Arenas rappelled onto the grass, holding the rope with one hand and their weapons in the other, firing full-auto as their bodies left the chopper. They landed on the grass and hit the ground, rolling in separate directions, changing magazines before switching to single-shot and shooting at the remaining mercenaries at the west wall. ATS shooters landed beside them, but then opposition reinforcements arrived. The mercenaries took positions shooting through gaps in the walls, or lying prone in the larger openings, laying down heavy fire. Axe tossed a frag grenade. As the detonation shook the ground, blasting shrapnel into the building, Arenas dropped smoke, and the big cloud billowed from the canister. He shouted for everybody to fall back to the tree line. Axe stayed by his right side as the shooters and Reapers Three and Four sought cover, Axe almost sliding too far down the slope, but stopping the progress with a foot on an extended branch.

One of the OCRTIS shooters shouted for Axe and

Arenas to provide covering fire while they broke out the rifle-grenades.

"Nice!" Axe shouted, sighting down the barrel of the HK 416. He zeroed on the part of a merc's head he could see through a hole in the wall. He fired once, twice. First shot hit the wall. The second shot scored. Axe watched the man fall. He shifted his aim.

Arenas emptied a magazine spraying controlled bursts in the direction of the enemy, the HK carbine chugging like a train as he sent 5.56mm hellfire downrange.

Return fire smacked into the grass, and the tree branches around them, bits of debris falling on Axe's neck as he reloaded. He was thankful for his combat goggles for keeping small bits of wood out of his eyes.

The three OCRTIS shooters stayed low, ignoring the incoming rounds, as they hurriedly attached long green snouts to the muzzles of their FAMAS F1 bullpup rifles.

The "snouts" had blunt ends and fins in the back. They were APAV 40 rifle-grenades, 40mm anti-personnel weapons of the fiercest caliber. Not only could it take down men, but armored vehicles too, if fired in the right spot. Discharged via a blank cartridge the OCRTIS shooters inserted into the firing chambers of their weapons, the three men took aim at the west wall and let the 40mm thunder fly.

The grenades smashed into the castle one, two, three, the explosions tremendous, Axe, Arenas, and the OCRTIS shooters dropping low to avoid the wash of flame and debris that came their way. Branches snapped and fell as chunks of rock struck, Axe felt something heavy land on his left leg. Looking up, Axe smiled at the gaping hole in the west wall, the clearing smoke, and the unobstructed entry into the interior.

"Move out!" he shouted, leading the charge. He heard the others behind him as he pounded across the grass and onto the concrete, where they had to slow to step around the biggest pieces of concrete debris. Stepping over a remaining portion of the west wall jutting from the floor level, Axe scanned for threats, then, seeing none, entered further. Arenas and the OCRTIS shooters spread out into what looked like a family room, with furniture, television, and kitchen off to one side.

Then Axe heard the noise.

As he turned to meet the threat, he decided some men are simply hard to kill.

Brick Peters and Pete Traynor rushed the porch, most of which had been conveniently destroyed in the first pass of the lead choppers blazing miniguns. But the upper floor above the porch was intact, with Reaper Five and Bravo Two forced to drop and roll across the hard ground to avoid the pair of mercs leaning out with their automatic weapons spitting death. The OCRTIS shooters behind them fired back and scattered, and then the first chopper swooped around for another pass, the miniguns cranking yet again, tracer fire resembling laser blasts vaporizing the window, the mercs, and the upper portion of the wall in an explosion of blood and concrete.

Brick coughed as he ran through the cloud of dust. Their entry into the castle was plainly available, but they had to climb over a rock pile to get inside. Brick led the charge, his big legs pumping as he stepped up and over the debris, reaching the interior with the HK 416 out and ready.

Movement ahead!

Brick shouted for everybody to get down as he met enemy troops head on. He fired the HK from the hip and dived right. No cover presented itself, so he landed on the dirty wood floor and kept rolling as enemy bullets impacted around him.

Ceasario Crisfulli finally climbed out from under the desk. He ignored the tremors throughout his body. He had Bella to protect.

Bella Lane carefully rose from behind the couch she'd jumped behind when the machine gun fire started, and, so far, hadn't let up. The salvos from the helicopters had done tremendous damage, even to the den, which was not directly over the porch, but close enough to feel the heat from the last minigun barrage. The walls in the den sprouted spider-cracks. Chandler, the mercenary captain, and Rosen had been in the next room shooting out the window. The machine gun blasts from the helicopter had certainly killed them both.

Crisfulli glanced at the door. The two bodies near the doorway, Adalene Severin and the mercenary who called himself Voltaire, might distract the assault force long enough for him to get a shot off at them. They might very well think the bodies belonged to him and Bella.

Crisfulli felt for the Beretta in the waistband of his slacks as he moved to the cabinet near the couch, grabbing for a Spectre M4, a stubby submachine gun from Italy. A loaded mag was already locked in place. He tossed the Spectre to Bella, who caught it and immediately checked the load. Crisfulli helped himself to another Spectre and pulled her over to the desk. They dropped behind it, positioned the chair to cover them further when Crisfulli stuck his head up to check the doorway.

Somebody had blasted through the roof to enter the second floor of the castle, that much Crisfulli knew. Where those commandos were right at that moment, he had no idea.

Bella Lane stayed low, both hands on the Spectre, her eyes darting around, but she said nothing.

Crisfulli almost felt a sense of relief when he heard his mercenaries charging up the stairs, their heavy boots more than obvious. He wanted to shout a warning that the intruders were waiting for them, but such a yell might give away his own position. If there was a way to escape, Crisfulli needed to find it. He only wished, then, that he hadn't blocked the tunnel exit. What was supposed to keep the White Wolf from escaping might have signed his, and Bella's, death warrants.

Kane counted six mercenary troops, decked out in combat black with chest rigs and heavy weapons, the rifle of choice being the SIG-Sauer SG540 in 7.62mm NATO. Kane tightened his grip on the Atchisson AA-12 shotgun.

The mercs climbed the staircase from the ground floor, but the landing forced them to turn right, with a railing blocking a left turn. Kane hid behind a wooden post supporting the ceiling, Cara at another post nearby, and Rigal and his OCRTIS shooters spread around elsewhere. The mercs cleared the steps, swinging right. Kane followed them with his eyes, noting they passed a hallway with an open door at the end, where it appeared two bodies lay in a puddle of blood.

Something to check later.

Kane shouted, "Now!" and lifted the AA-12.

Boom boom — sweep left — *boom boom.*

The double-ought buck flashing from the AA-12's muzzle joined the crackles of assault rifle fire, a pair of mercs falling to the first burst. The second burst missed, shredding part of the railing instead, but nicking a merc in the leg and causing him to tumble to the floor. He scrambled out of the way, avoiding a burst from Cara that would have cut him in half.

Kane ducked back as return fire struck the support post and turned to rubbish trim pieces along the wall, the nasty 7.62mm bullets replacing the trim with holes big enough to cram a fist into.

Kane shifted to the opposite side of the post, joining Cara in another salvo, empty brass clattering at their feet. The French shooters added to the mix, and dead mercs fell into the paths of their compatriots, causing a tumble of arms and legs and weapons near the stairway exit.

Kane lowered the shotgun long enough to assess. As wounded-but-still-fighting mercs struggled to rise, Kane shouted for Cara. Reapers One and Two charged across the open space, Rigal and the OCRTIS shooters covering them. Kane squeezed the AA-12's trigger, spending every shell in the full-auto shotgun's magazines, chopping the mercs like trees in a forest brought down by a trio of multi-blade buzz saws.

Kane wanted to go down the hall.

Kane dropped the AA-12 on the floor and grabbed the HK 416 from behind his back. Snapping back the action to chamber a round, he moved forward. Despite Cara's calls to wait, Kane stepped over the bodies to approach the open doorway. Quickly she caught up to him as Rigal radioed they'd continue searching the floor. Kane acknowledged. He took one side of the hallway, Cara the other.

"What do you think is down there?"

"Somebody."

"Crisfulli?"

"Maybe."

"Who're the bodies?"

"Let's find out."

Kane plucked a smoke grenade from his chest rig and rolled it down the hall. White smoke hissed from the canister as he traveled the length of the hallway, the canister bumping against the shoulder of the dead woman in the doorway and ricocheting into the room.

A barrage of full-auto fire answered the smoke, but the un-aimed blast turned the wall near Kane into a pock-marked moonscape that took down a painting and shattered a vase.

Kane left the wall to join Cara.

"I think Crisfulli's in there," he said.

"If so, he has no way out," Cara said.

Kane said, "Let's end this."

"Right behind you."

Axe Burton tried to bring his HK to bear, but the big merc charging him hit him hard, grabbing his legs above the knee to bring him down. Axe landed on his right shoulder. The debris scattered across the floor made the touchdown much more painful than it might otherwise have been.

More gunfire crackled around him as more mercenaries arrived, Arenas and the OCRTIS shooters engaging.

Axe was on his own.

For now.

The merc let go of Axe's legs long enough to throw a punch combination at Reaper Four's face. Axe blocked one. The other connected solidly with his face, the blow punishing, Axe's vision spinning as he felt more impacts. He kept his arms up, deflecting most of the strikes. Then the merc reached for his belt, grabbing a long-bladed knife. Axe's right hand snaked to the holster on his thigh, grabbing his SIG pistol. He brought the gun up, at the same time he wedged his left leg between him and the merc, pushing the big man away. Extended the SIG, Axe fired two shots into the man's chest, then followed with a shot through the merc's forehead. The merc's body ceased movement as if somebody had thrown a switch. He collapsed to the ground.

Axe laughed. "Told you it works, Cara," he said to himself.

Axe rolled right, switching the SIG to his left hand while he grabbed the HK with his right. Staying on the ground, he scrambled for the concealment of a large display stand against a wall, the ceramic art pieces resting on top already half gone from bullet strikes.

"Reaper Four, Reaper Three, where you at?"

"Hiding behind a big vase." Axe holstered the SIG and tucked the HK into his shoulder. A bullet slammed into the wall inches from his face, and he ducked back.

There was quite a party going on. Arenas and the OCRTIS shooters were pinned behind furniture, firing on a crew of mercs who weren't shrinking in number. In fact, more troops joined them, and Axe spotted four in a hurried conference, possibly planning a rush.

Axe sighted on the man doing the talking and fired once. His head snapped back. The other three scrambled for cover, Axe laying down a pattern of fire that took out one more before the final two found a place to hide.

Arenas said over the com unit, "Grenades!"

"Got your back," Axe said, slinging the HK to grab the frag grenades from his belt. He pulled the pin on one, held the spoon. When Arenas gave the order, he tossed at the same time as Reaper Three. Axe pulled the pin on a second grenade and flung that after the first.

He drew back behind the wall.

The explosions shook the room, knocking off anything still hanging on the walls, shrapnel flying in all directions. But the shooting stopped.

Axe wiped his goggles and looked around the corner.

The bodies of the mercs were spread everywhere, arms and legs every which way. The only thing Axe knew for sure was that nobody in that pile was moving.

"Keep moving," Axe said, leaving his hiding spot to join Arenas and the OCRTIS shooters. They continued forward. They still had plenty of enemy troops to clean out.

Brick scrambled through a doorway on his left as automatic weapons fire hammered behind him. He looked up. The kitchen. Tiled floor, center island, countertop all around.

"Brick!"

"In the kitchen, Traynor!"

A door across the room opened. Three more mercenaries emerged. The trio stopped in surprise as Brick rose to meet them, the HK 416 tracking the lead shooter. Brick fired once. The merc fell back, his two buddies dropping behind the center island. Brick bent into a squat, slowly beginning a circle of the island. A head popped up. Brick fired, dropped lower as one of the mercs shot at him. Brick moved faster, the other footsteps equaling his speed. When Brick rounded the opposite side, the last thing he saw was the boot of one of the mercs as they rounded the corner opposite.

That's when they ran into Pete Traynor, in the doorway Brick had entered through. Traynor's HK spit flame. Brick ran to him, and both mercs were dead on the floor.

"Waste of good tile," Traynor said.

"Where's the boss?"

Traynor said into his com unit, "Bravo Two, Reaper One. Status?"

No response.

"Reaper One, do you copy?"

Kane moved quickly along the wall, Cara behind him, the smoke finally dissipating, but some of it still lingering in the hallway.

They reached the corner and stopped, the doorway only a few steps away. Voices within the room. Panic. A man and a woman.

Kane let the HK fall on its sling and chucked in a grenade.

The blast rocked the wall.

Cara left the wall, moving in a half-circle to clear a little of the door at a time. She made a fist with her left hand. Kane moved forward, turning sharply into the office with Cara right behind him.

The grenade blast had wiped out a lot of the room, but the big desk in the center had barely been touched. There was one body on the floor, a red-headed woman, and the man rising from behind the desk, his white suit covered in blood, wore a snarl that showed Kane he wasn't leaving the present world without taking somebody with him.

Kane and Cara fired at the same time, their HKs

popping as the single shots left the barrels. Ceasario Crisfulli never fired a shot, the 5.56mm tumblers tearing through the fabric of his suit to rip through flesh and bone. He fell backward, hitting the wall behind, then settling onto the carpet.

"Reaper One, do you copy?"

Kane lowered his weapon to respond.

"Reaper Three, Reaper One. Top floor. Crisfulli is down. Repeat, Crisfulli is down."

CHAPTER 18

Presently, the surviving mercenaries gave up. Despite Rigal's decision not to take prisoners, he had his shooters round up the mercs and sit them in the grass outside.

"You got Crisfulli?" Rigal asked Kane.

John Kane sat against an outer wall that had escaped damage. Cara sat with him. Kane jumped up to meet Rigal's eyes.

"We did. Grenade blast got his girlfriend. Billings and me got him."

"Good. It's over then."

"This time."

Rigal patted Kane on the shoulder. "This time is all I'm thinking about right now, my friend."

Rigal walked away to consult with some of his shooters, who were standing nearby.

Cara stood up.

"That's good advice, Reaper."

"What is?"

"One battle at a time."

"Maybe he's right."

. . .

Team Reaper Headquarters
El Paso, TX

John Kane did not look away as the eyes of General Mary Thurston and Luis Ferrero bored into him.

They sat in Ferrero's office. Thurston had wanted to have the meeting there with Ferrero present. Kane wished they had met in Thurston's office because the fluorescent bulbs above their heads needed changing, and flickered on and off. Kane wasn't sure what he hated more. Cartels, or fluorescent bulbs on the fritz.

"What are we supposed to do with you, Reaper?" Thurston asked. She sat beside Ferrero's desk, with Zero himself directly behind it. The cluttered desk between them meant nothing to Kane, despite the fact that his superiors were trying to create a block between him and them. Typical. They wanted him to remove the block. Symbolically, of course, although Kane figured he'd have little trouble shoving the desk to one side should that effort ever be required.

"I apologize for my behavior, ma'am. I'm a little tired."

"Tired of what?" Ferrero asked.

"Banging my head against the wall."

"We're *all* tired of that, Reaper," Ferrero said. "I myself am particularly wiped out. But I still show up for work every day."

"Uh-huh."

"Your insubordination is unacceptable, Reaper," Thurston said.

"You're right."

"That's all you have to say?" the general asked.

"I've apologized. I'm not going to grovel. I was having a bad time, I explained why, and that has passed. Unless you're firing me, I'm not leaving this unit."

"You exhaust me," the general said, shaking her head.

Kane grinned.

"What's so funny?"

"My mother," Kane said, "once had a big lecture prepared for me over something or other. She wasn't expecting me to admit anything, and it took the wind out of her sail."

"You think this chat has made me less mad, Reaper?"

"All I know is I'm not getting a lecture."

Thurston opened her mouth to respond, but Ferrero cut her off with a raised hand.

He said, "Get your ass out of my office, Reaper."

Kane didn't have to be told twice.

Don Mateo answered the call on the third ring.

"Hey, Don."

"Johnny, how's it going?"

"Have you adjusted back to civilian life?"

"Nuts, you should meet my new client. You all right?"

"We're good. All intact. I thought you'd like to know that little thing in Nassau has been resolved."

"Find the money?"

"No, but we killed most of the guys who were paid with it."

Don Mateo laughed. "Very good. Katie sends her love."

"Tell her same from me."

"Where are you now?"

"Home in Texas. Well, at headquarters. Paperwork and all that."

"Don't miss it."

"I'm going to try and get away from here for a couple of weeks, boss's orders," Kane said. "How long will you be with your client?"

"Give me a few days. Shouldn't take much longer."

"Great. I need a rest."

"I can hear it in your voice, buddy. Take care."

Paperwork and debriefing finally ended after the sun went down. Kane, worn out but still wide awake, exited the building. He considered the operation against the French-Italian Corridor a successful failure, in that far more damage had been done than they were able to prevent, but at least he'd kept his friends alive. He looked forward to seeing Don and Katie again, and very soon.

He'd learned that Bascomb, the ocean explorer, was back to teaching classes, the incident with him and his family quietly swept aside by British authorities and his university. The two men Crisfulli had left in London, still in custody, were talking, telling MI5 everything they knew about the Corridor and its operations. The Brits were feeding the information back to Team Reaper, and, so far, Sam Swift had been able to confirm the data with what he was learning from the cell phone hacks.

Xavier Rigal and his OCRTIS people were taking over the effort of rounding up the small fry, based on Reaper's intelligence. Kane wanted no part of that. He found it amusing, though, when Slick had mentioned all the little pushers and drug thugs running for the hills. Their mistake?

They kept their cell phones with them. OCRTIS was right behind them all the way.

Kane approached his truck, looking forward to bed and the coming R&R that he needed to figure out.

He'd made it halfway across the parking lot when he heard an engine rev and Axe yell his name.

Axe and Arenas and Brick were in Axe's SUV, Brick leaning out the passenger side window.

"What are you guys up to?" Kane asked.

"Bowling."

"Again?"

"It's fun, Reaper!" Axe said.

"He likes the girl who gives out the shoes," Brick said.

Kane shook his head.

"Come along," Arenas said from the back seat.

"I'll follow you."

"None of that crap," Axe said. "We got room, hop in."

Kane smiled and went around the side of the SUV, jumping in back behind Axe.

Axe drove out of the parking lot.

"Cara meeting us there?" Kane asked.

"Cara and Pete, yeah," said Arenas.

"I should warn you guys; I'm a very good bowler."

The other men laughed.

"Seriously. My parents made me take classes in 1983. I won a trophy."

"We need proof," Axe said. "Still have it?"

Kane admitted he did not.

IF YOU LIKED LETHAL TENDER, YOU MIGHT ENJOY THE TERMINATION PROTOCOL (SCOTT STILETTO BOOK 1)

BY BRIAN DRAKE

The Termination Protocol is the first book in the hard-edged, action thriller series – Scott Stiletto.

The United States is under siege, and the enemy has help from the White House!

Scott Stiletto is one of the CIA's toughest assets, a veteran of numerous missions, an operative with compassion and ruthlessness in equal parts.

His enemy is the New World Revolutionary Front, a terrorist organization seeking to overthrow the government of the United States and install their own puppet--a willing puppet, who is already very close to the president he wishes to replace.

With freedom and justice hanging in the balance, Scott Stiletto gives no quarter. He will give the enemy a one-way ticket to hell!

"...99% pure action fun, no additives. I had

to stop reading the book several times just to catch my breath..."

AVAILABLE NOW

ABOUT THE AUTHOR

A twenty-five year veteran of radio and television broadcasting, **Brian Drake** has spent his career in San Francisco where he's filled writing, producing, and reporting duties with stations such as KPIX-TV, KCBS, KQED, among many others.

Currently carrying out sports and traffic reporting duties for Bloomberg 960, Brian Drake spends time between reports and carefully guarded morning and evening hours cranking out action/adventure tales. A love of reading when he was younger inspired him to create his own stories, and he sold his first short story, "The Desperate Minutes," to an obscure webzine when he was 25 (more years ago than he cares to remember, so don't ask). Many more short story sales followed before he expanded to novels, entering the self-publishing field in 2010, and quickly building enough of a following to attract the attention of several publishers and other writing professionals.

Brian Drake lives in California with his wife and two cats, and when he's not writing he is usually blasting along the back roads in his Corvette with his wife telling him not to drive so fast, but the engine is so loud he usually can't hear her.

For more information:
https://wolfpackpublishing.com/brian-drake/

Printed in Great Britain
by Amazon

65697745R00154